Haunted by Murder

The Mag and Clara Balefire Mysteries

BOOK FOUR

REGINA WELLING
ERIN LYNN

Haunted by Murder

ISBN- 978-1-953044-11-2

Cover design by: L. Vryhof

Interior design by: L. Vryhof

http://reginawelling.com

http://erinlynnwrites.com

First Edition

Printed in the U.S.A.

Contents

Chapter One

"Two hundred." Hawk-sharp eyes set in the face of a kindly grandmother gave Margaret Balefire an unfair advantage. People rarely saw her coming, and with her skills, she could haggle the halo off an angel.

"One fifty." Her opponent, a buttoned-up type with close-cropped hair and a condescending air countered, but she could tell he was good for a bit more.

"One seventy-five and not a penny less," Mag fired back.

After a moment of watching her for signs of weakness, the customer swallowed her deceptively dainty hand in his, and sealed the deal.

"You won't be sorry, and your wife will love adding this to her collection." Turning, Mag winked at her sister, Clara, who returned the saucy gesture in kind despite the fact she was now on the hook for a lobster dinner.

When the bell over the door jingled behind the happy customer, Mag let out a witch-worthy cackle, and did the old-lady version of a booty dance.

"Told you I'd sell that French boudoir doll before the end of the week," she told Clara, smirking. "You should never bet against me; I'm a sure thing."

Driving a hard bargain rated one of the top spots on Mag's list of fun things to do. Just above scoring one off her sister, but below kicking the butt of anyone or anything that deserved it. With magic, naturally.

"It's not polite to gloat," Clara replied, "though I'll admit you earned the win. That was the creepiest doll I have ever seen in my life." And that included a nasty little poppet gifted to her from none other than Marie Laveau during Clara's one and only trip to New Orleans.

"Ernestine?" Mag scoffed. "She's a beauty. That auburn hair, those painted eyes. Did you see the pin tucks in her dress, and the handmade lace? Sure, she had a few worn places, but who doesn't when they're coming up on ninety years old?"

Clara paused in her end of the day cleaning to consider. "It was the eyes that gave me the heebies. They're crooked." She waved the feather duster at Mag. Anything that stared in two different directions at the same time was not to be trusted.

"Hand painted," Mag countered.

"They followed me around the shop, and I—" Whatever Clara had been about to say was lost in the aftermath of a violent shiver. "Did you feel that?" She craned her head around to see if the A/C unit had kicked on, but all the lights were out, and the plug dangled below the outlet.

Mag huffed a breath out through her nose. "It was just a doll, Clarie. Not the spawn of Chucky."

"Don't you even joke about a thing like that," she said, glowering. A fan of horror movies, Clara was not. Just one more difference between the Balefire sisters.

It gave her no sense of triumph, then, when Mag shivered, skittered to the side, and stared at the spot where an icy wind had just washed not only over her, but through her.

"Okay," Mag said, rubbing her arms and glancing around the room. "That *was* weird."

A history spanning more than two human lifetimes spent pursuing rogue magic in beast form had provided Mag with a unique and deeply personal perspective on the term weird.

The bell over the door jangled and the unsettling experience faded into the background then was forgotten as the business day wore on.

Balms and Bygones, a store as unique as its owners, allowed the sisters to combine Mag's love of all things old with Clara's knack for creating personal care products. Polished to a shine, Mag's carefully-chosen shelves and cabinets made the perfect showcase for the jewel-toned bottles and jars that held Clara's wares.

Located on the edges of Harmony, a coastal resort community, the shop enjoyed a spillover of tourism, which the Balefire sisters didn't mind at all. Even if they had to hide their inherent witchiness from most of the locals as part of the bargain.

"I'm telling you, it's like magic." A vivacious redhead assured her shopping companion. "I'm wearing sandals in public without shame, and my heels are as soft as a baby's behind. First time that's happened in years."

She turned wide blue eyes on Clara. "You have a website I can order from? Because if you don't, I'll give you fair warning: I'm going to clean you out. We only come up this way once a year, and I'll need to stock up."

"We do." Clara handed over a brochure, then watched with fascination as the woman whirled through the shop enthusiastically filling a basket anyway. Mag's lobster winnings wouldn't take much of a bite out of her half of the day's profits. Cha-ching.

"I'm May, this is my cousin's wife, Cindy. She's local, but I'm the one who found this place first." As she chattered, more things landed in the basket while Cindy merely nodded, and turned away to stare out the front window.

Shy, or maybe not into shopping, Cindy hunched her shoulders in the way some willowy women do when they're feeling taller than everyone else and want to fade into the woodwork. Her back to the room, she stood with thin arms folded over her chest and let the conversation swirl into the space without her.

"Do you market your line to salons at all?" May asked, tossing a couple more items into the basket. "My pedicurist is going to flip when she sees my feet, and I bet she'll want to buy in bulk. Maybe you'd better give me some more of those brochures. Does this purifying mask come in a larger size?"

"Yes—" Clara managed before May pelted her with another barrage of questions.

Maybe Cindy wasn't shy—maybe she simply knew she wouldn't get a word in edgewise with May around, and resigned herself to silence.

Fascinated, Mag slid onto one of the tall stools and rested her elbow on the counter and her chin in her hand to watch what happened next. Once, Cindy swiveled her head enough for Mag to catch a subtle eye-roll.

"Oh, that lemongrass-and-sage bath salt smells divine." May discovered the tester shelf and opened every container for either a sniff or to try a dab on her skin. The woman smelled like a bushel of herbs in a flower garden by the time she got through the lot. But, to Clara's delight, she continued adding items to her basket.

"Doesn't this smell amazing?" Hustling over toward the window, May shoved the un-stoppered container in Cindy's face.

"It's nice, I guess." A delicate shudder shook Cindy's shoulders, and Mag saw the wave of gooseflesh crawl across the woman's skin. "I'll be out front, you take your time, though." Her smile carried a hint of warmth, but her eyes refused to meet Mag's. It was obvious Cindy didn't want to be there.

"I'm sorry. She's a really nice person, but she's not very outgoing. I had to drag her out of the house or she'd never have come here at all." Apology over, May returned to her shopping.

When she couldn't squeeze another tube or bottle into her basket, she headed to the register and didn't even flinch at the number Clara quoted when she rang in the final item. "I'm just going to grab another container of that lemongrass bath salt for Cindy, and then I think that will do it."

"It's on the house, and we'll gift wrap it for you." Clara said we, but she meant Mag since her sister was sitting in front of the gift-wrapping area. Despite her gruff demeanor, Mag found a certain Zen-like satisfaction in the precise nature of folding paper to create a pretty package.

She wrapped the jar in tissue paper the color of a tropical sea, creating soft pleats along the sides. Mag was tucking a few sprigs of lavender into the fan shape at the top, when cool air crept over her fingers, and this time, there was more. Her fingers fumbled when a sense of being watched sent a tingle up the nape of her neck, lifting all the tiny hairs to prickling attention.

More than six months they'd been running this shop, and she'd never felt anything like that before. Surreptitiously, she called on the magical Balefire from which the sisters derived their last name, and dropped her hands below the countertop to let it hover unseen over her skin. The warmth pushed back the lingering chill.

Working quickly, she threaded a length of cheery, yellow ribbon through the handle of a small wooden scoop, affixed the scoop to the top of the package, and handed the salts back to Clara.

"If you'll excuse me," Mag said, "I need to check on something." She felt Clara's puzzled gaze on her back, but kept going.

The building that housed Balms and Bygones rambled back from the storefront through a doorway and into a space magically enhanced to more than double its original size.

The front section of the back room contained Clara's workshop, where she brewed and tested her wares. Mag restored furniture in the rear portion. Boxes of product, crates of knick-knacks, and boxes of seasonal merchandise took up the rest of the space.

When Clara walked in several minutes later expecting to see an empty room, Mag stood in the middle of her workshop, unmoving.

"What's wrong, Maggie?" The question startled Mag and she jumped. "You've been gone so long, I thought you went home."

"Don't sneak up on me like that. I'm old; you'll give me a heart attack. Is she gone?" Craning her neck around, Mag glanced back through the doorway to see the open sign now flipped to closed. "What happened? Did Mrs. Moneybags buy you out?"

"May?" Frowning, Clara said, "She left half an hour ago, and I closed up the shop. Is something wrong? Have you been standing here this whole time?" Heart thumping against her rib cage, she searched Mag's face for signs of illness or pain. Seeing neither, Clara released a relieved sigh.

"Seems like," Mag replied, her attention elsewhere. "Got any white sage in your supplies?"

Like any good alchemist, Clara kept her workstation neat. A ruthlessly organized set of shelves held paper bags full of dried herbs labeled in permanent marker. It took only seconds for her to locate the container of sage and set it on the table while Mag rifled through cabinets.

"Where are the smudge pots? I can't find anything the way you keep changing things around." The normally unflappable Mag seemed pretty flapped. "This place is overdue for a good cleansing. Get me the salt, too, while you're at it."

Nudging past her sister, Clara picked up on the radiating tension.

"Is this about Hagatha's no-cursing charm again? We've searched the place from top to bottom. It has to be in the walls."

Mag shook her head, some of her focus still on the aura of the room. "This isn't Hagatha's doing, I don't think. It feels different, but I suppose she could be up to something. Honestly, I'm not sure why she decided to sell this place and move."

While she considered the devious mind and possible intentions of the store's former owner—an old witch named Hagatha Crow—Mag piled sage leaves into the bowl of a smudge pot and plucked an ember from the Balefire.

Taking more than just her last name from the source of witch's magic, Mag could have crawled into the fireplace and felt nothing more than a pleasant tingle on her skin: one of the perks of being born a Balefire, the family that guarded and fed the sacred flame, a responsibility handed down through the generations.

"I'm sure she had a reason." Taking a second smudge pot and using a feather to direct the smoke, Clara followed her sister back into the shop and peeled off in the opposite direction to get the job done faster. The scent of burning sage tickled her nose as it spread through the space. "And I'm just as certain I don't want to know what it was. We're in too deep with her already, and she's been suspiciously quiet since her trip to the Faelands. I don't want to buy trouble, but we both know a quiet Hagatha is a—"

The rest of the sentence went right out of Clara's head when an eerie keening split the air—the kind of sound that vibrated along her back teeth and set them on edge. A rumble echoed up from deep beneath the floorboards, and the old house quivered like the skin on a cow's flank when she twitches to dislodge a biting fly.

A slow, rolling wave of electricity crawled along Clara's skin and crackled across her scalp, sending her hair floating around her head. Her ears popped under a sudden heavy pressure, and the air misted, turning the light in the room an eerie shade of green.

Mag's smudge pot hit the floor with a resounding crash and spilled embers onto wooden floorboards unprotected by the Balefire affinity. The scent of hot wax and charring wood smeared the air as Clara shook off the shock and wrapping her fingers around the burning coals, added them to her own pot.

"That's going to leave a mark," she said, shaking her fingers. While in no actual danger of the Balefire burning the place down as long as one of the sisters was there to exert control, fire was fire and if the hungry flames saw a chance to take a taste of polished oak, they would. "What just happened?"

Mag never answered, and when Clara looked up, she figured out why.

A thin haze of smoke curled and clung to a hovering, vaguely human-shaped figure. A ghost. In Balms and Bygones. No wonder Hagatha had sold the place to them for a ridiculous sum.

"Hello, Roma." Or not, since Mag recognized the spirit and greeted her warmly. "Uh. Sorry for your …

What, she wondered, was the proper protocol for expressing condolences *to* the newly dead?

Chapter Two

Smoothing down her prematurely white flyaway hair, Mag gave the ghost her due. "You always did know how to make an entrance."

"It's about time you clued in," the ghost said, crossing her arms and staring until Mag squirmed. "I've been trying to get through to you for days. Didn't you learn anything from our lessons, Maggie?"

The use of the nickname tipped Clara off that there was history between the two women, and piqued her curiosity to the breaking point.

The sisters had followed vastly different paths in life. After two and a half centuries, Clara was painfully aware there was a lifetime's worth of experiences separating them, and she knew little of her sister's adventures. She didn't need to know every missed detail, but when an opportunity to close the gap came knocking on her door—or, in this case, invaded without invitation—Clara had every intention of siphoning whatever bits of information she could glean.

Coming to her senses, Mag made a proper introduction. "Roma, this is my sister, Clara. Clara, meet

Roma, an old friend of mine." Clara lurched, preparing to shake the woman's hand before a mental Captain Obvious smacked her in the face and pointed out that there would be nothing to hold onto. "Roma is—was—the best medium in New England."

"It's very nice to meet you, Roma, though I'd say the circumstances are less than ideal." Clara's tone held a tentative mix of warmth and uncertainty.

Roma's booming laugh shook the walls. The contents of one shelf nearly tumbled to the floor before Mag calmly loosed a flicker of magic and set everything back to rights.

"No, dear," Roma said, pivoting toward Clara. "I'd say my circumstances are quite dire. I find myself in the unenviable position of needing my own services." If ghosts could blush, Roma's face might have tinted a delicate pink.

"Mag has mentioned you many times. It's nice to finally put a face to the name." Roma appraised Clara with the unfair advantage of having more information about her than Clara had about Roma, a dynamic that made the younger Balefire sister more than a little uncomfortable. For Hecate's sake, this whole experience made Clara more than a little uncomfortable, but she'd be damned if she'd let either Roma or her sister smell any hint of weakness.

"Let's dispense with the pleasantries, Roma. What are you doing here? Why didn't you cross over?" Mag demanded, crossing her arms and quickly cutting to the crux of the problem in true Margaret Balefire style. "You of all people ought to know the dangers of sticking around the land of the living for too long."

Roma began to pace the floor, each step causing a swirl of dust-like mist to curl around her feet. "Well, obviously I have some unfinished business, and I've wasted too much time trying to talk to any of the frustratingly-inept mediums in the area. I think I gave Madame Roselda over in Tewksbury quite a fright, though." The ghostly chuckle chilled the air.

"She thinks she's just a scam artist. Been fooling people for years without realizing she actually did have the gift." Roma shook her head and rolled her eyes. "How was I supposed to know she was the one moving the planchette across the board? I gave it a nudge, and you'd have thought I'd electrocuted her or something. She tried to leave a Roselda-shaped hole in the door."

Another chuckle breezed in Clara's direction and Mag let out a snort.

"Then it hit me that I was focusing my efforts in the wrong direction, and that's when I remembered seeing your photo in the paper. I have to say, I was surprised to see the mighty Raythe-hunting Margaret Balefire participating in a small-town flotilla race. But as I continued reading, it became clear you had an ulterior motive. Solved a murder, didn't you?"

It hadn't started out that way, but Mag wasn't about to ruin her reputation and cop to joining the race just to get free advertising for Balms and Bygones. "Yes, we did."

"Good. I'm glad to see you're keeping your skills honed. And now I need to make use of your investigative abilities. There's another crime that needs solving."

Mag raised an eyebrow. "Does this have anything to do with your death?" She minced no words.

"My death?" Roma let loose another trilling laugh. "No, I wasn't murdered. I just happened to wake up dead the other morning. Took me a moment to realize it, but I'll tell you I'm not lamenting the loss of my aching hips."

Asking any woman her age is a no-no, but looking at her, Clara would have put Roma in the ninety-something range.

"Being dead is positively pain-free, and once this whole business has been wrapped up I'll happily follow the light and find out what comes next."

"You know I'll help if I'm able," Max said. "Never been one to turn down a challenge, that's for sure." She cast a quick glance at her sister and was relieved to see Clara nodding her agreement, even if her motivation stemmed from the desire to rid the house of a talkative old ghost rather than help one of her sister's old friends.

The Balefire sisters settled into chairs around the table that held Mag's favorite crystal ball and waited for Roma to jump into the story. Instead, the old ghost gave a pointed glance at the table, and then at Mag.

"Lost, eh?"

So rarely did Mag find herself on the receiving end of a well-deserved dressing down, her face flushed a dull red, and she mumbled an apology in hopes of staving off the tirade. "I meant to give it back."

"What am I missing?" Clara looked from one to the other.

"This"—Roma reached to touch the crystal and then made a face when her hand went right through it—"was my great aunt Lavinia's second favorite crystal ball, the one she used when she taught me to gaze. Many an hour I've spent peering into its depths. I loaned it to Margaret last year. She was supposed to use it until she bought a new one, but she never gave it back."

A lesser woman might have quailed under Roma's unflinching stare, but Mag only grinned. "I never bought a new one, so technically, the loan is still valid. If you needed it, you could have asked for it back. It's a fine piece, though. Just the right size, nearly perfect clarity, and that pale golden hue doesn't put strain on the eyes. I never found the like of it, and I've looked."

Roma lifted a shoulder. "I suppose it can't be helped now. It's not like I can take it with me. Use it well, and with my blessing. Now, can we get on with why I'm here?"

Since she couldn't take a seat herself, Roma continued her painless pacing while delving into the reason she'd made contact.

"I know you haven't lived in Harmony for long, but you must have heard of the Huffington family by now, no?" Roma asked.

"Yes, of course." Clara replied. "Huffington Manor is that big white place with the columns out front, just before you pitch down into the valley. I've seen the name listed as donor for about a dozen different charities. So far, though, I haven't crossed paths with any of the family."

"That's partly because there aren't many of them left. Just Stephanie, the only child of the last male heir. Kennedy Huffington and his wife Josephine were killed about fifteen years ago in a tragic car accident."

Giving a sympathetic head shake, Roma told the sad tale. "Kennedy died instantly, but Jo wasn't wearing her seat belt. She went through the windshield, but that wasn't the worst of it."

Her sympathies already engaged, Clara wasn't sure she wanted to hear the rest.

"They had a daughter named Stephanie who was in the back seat and she saw the whole thing. When the authorities arrived, they found her cradling her mother's body. She was bruised and shaken, but otherwise unharmed. Such a traumatic experience."

"What happened to her? The girl, I mean."

"She went to live with Kennedy's sister, Buffy."

"Wait, you're telling me there's a Buffy Huffington out there?" Despite the gravity of the situation, Mag just couldn't let that one go.

Roma shot her a quelling look, "Not anymore. Huffington was her maiden name, and she was married by then. Anyway, she passed away two years ago. Now it's just Stephanie and Buffy's husband, John Masters, and there's a cousin from Jo's side of the family, but I guess she doesn't count as a Huffington, so technically, Stephanie is the last in line."

The poor thing, Clara thought, *so young to have seen so much tragedy.*

"Anyhow, Josephine was a client of mine. Lots of them had the sight in her line, gypsy people they were, but not a breath of the gift in her. So, every month like clockwork she'd show up for a reading."

Roma shook her head and her voice pitched lower, "Pity she didn't always listen, or she might still be alive. Used to bring Stephanie with her, and the girl had a little something in the way of talent. Raw and unfocused, but a good base."

Mag circled a hand at Roma to hurry the story along and then shivered when the dead psychic directed a chilling blast her way.

"Once Jo died," Roma continued, casting glare at her old friend, "I figured I'd never see Stephanie again. Not if Buffy had any say. But then, it must have been six or seven years later, she showed up on my doorstep a grown woman, and I swear, for a solid thirty seconds I thought she was her mother's ghost." Roma stopped talking, her already misty eyes shimmering at the memory.

"So what's the mystery?" Mag asked, impatient.

"Do you have somewhere else to be, Margaret? Something more important to do? Always one step ahead and raring to go. But this is probably the last story I'm going to get to tell, and I'll take as long as I please."

Very few people had the guts to stand up to her sister like that, and Clara wished she'd had a chance to meet the living version of Roma and pry a few Mag stories out of her in private. An admiring smile played around her lips.

"Stephanie picked up right where Josephine left off, dropping in on a regular basis to seek guidance from the spirit realm. Never could get her parents to come through, though I know that's what she hoped for. I told her it's better to know they've moved on and found peace, but I know she still fostered hope. People do sometimes."

Clara caught the look that Roma flickered toward Mag and glanced over to see her sister flinch just a little. Who had her sister been unable to contact? One more question for the Secrets of Mag file.

"About a year ago, Stephanie met a man named Brad and I saw the cobwebs lift for the first time since the accident. The happy just glowed out of her, and about six months later, she got engaged. My guides approved the match, and I thought her future was secure."

Roma ignored the sigh Mag heaved and finally got to the crux of the matter.

"Then, about a week ago, Stephanie showed up looking like she'd been run over by a truck. Brad had packed up and left town with no warning, no goodbye, nothing but a lousy note that didn't explain a thing. Stephanie couldn't accept it. Too familiar, I think, the feeling of abandonment. She insisted he would never do something like that, and I could see the internal struggle raging inside her. I also sensed danger."

Roma stopped talking, and looked expectantly toward Mag. "Aren't you going to ask what the danger was?"

"I was keeping my lips zipped, like you told me to, Roma." Came Mag's passive-aggressive reply. "And I'm assuming you don't know, or you wouldn't be here."

"Well, you're right about that." Roma allowed. "But I think Stephanie felt it too. She said she'd been having nightmares that didn't feel like dreams, and was beginning to doubt her own sanity. I know it's not much to go on, but I didn't have a chance to delve any further and now I'm basically useless. That's where you come in."

Paws thundered on the stairs and two cats burst into the back room of the shop with their tails all puffed up and their backs arched. Neither one batted an eye at Roma's indistinct form.

Seeing no one else around, Pyewacket shrugged off her Siamese cat form as if it were a coat she wore. And maybe it was. If there was an origin story for how familiars gained the ability to slip from cat to human and back again, they kept it a tightly-guarded secret.

All tawny and golden and annoyed, Pye fixed her crystal-blue gaze on her bonded companion, Clara. "There's a ghost dog upstairs, and it will not stop barking." She jerked her head toward Jinx, still in cat form, and sitting on Mag's feet. "You know how he gets around dogs."

At the beginning of summer, Mrs. Green, the neighbor from two houses down, had added a few goldfish to the water feature in her backyard. Fascinated, Jinx had taken to sneaking over and watching them swim in lazy circles. Then Mrs. Green's daughter dropped off little Harley, a miniature schnauzer with a huge personality. Harley had only been defending his territory from an intruder when his sudden barking startled Jinx so badly he fell into the pond.

It might have been an easier sell if Harley hadn't decided Jinx needed rescuing and jumped in after him. In the end, Clara had to yank the wet dog and the wet cat out of the pond and conjure two more fish to replace the ones that hadn't survived the kerfuffle.

Since then, Jinx developed a twitch every time he heard a dog bark.

"I assume he's with you." Both a statement and a question directed toward Roma in Mag's driest tone.

Roma looked anywhere but at Mag. "His name is Whizzer, and it's a delicate situation."

The sound of his name must have carried up the stairs, because Whizzer came running. He skidded around the corner straight toward Roma, who instinctively took a step back even though she was in no danger of being knocked over by the spectral beast.

Losing her balance, Roma crumpled like a piece of paper and landed on her butt, smack dab in the middle of the Balefire. For a split second, a panicked look crossed her face, but when she realized there was no harm done besides her essence turning a lovely shade of purple, Roma let out a laugh and hopped to her feet.

Jinx, however, climbed Mag's leg and earned himself a reprimand nearly as sharp as his claws before he took the hint and changed to human form.

"Stop," he commanded as soon as he'd changed. His voice rang with authority, and Whizzer obeyed. Dropping to ghostly haunches, the Labrador retriever sat and stared up at Jinx with adoring eyes, his tongue lolling out the side of his mouth.

"I think he likes you." The man's voice coming from right behind her—a little too close if anyone had asked her, though no one did—made Clara's heart lurch and she took a hasty step forward. And then she felt like a jerk. What if the ghost thought he'd scared her? Well, he *did* scare her, but not in the there's-a-ghost-and-now-I'm-creeped-out way.

Really, how terrifying could he be? She turned to look at him, and it was just as she'd suspected: he looked like a slightly transparent, middle-aged accountant.

Silence fell over the strange tableau while the four living contemplated the three dead, and continued until Whizzer lived up to his name by casually strolling over to Clara's workbench and lifting his leg to loose a stream of doggy ectoplasm all over the upright support.

Pyewacket wrinkled her nose and still managed to come off looking regal. It was one of her gifts—probably something to do with her feline pedigree.

"Is there something you want to tell me, Roma?" Having more history with the medium and her methods, Mag had picked up on some nuance of the situation that had gone right past her sister.

Roma's feet, clad in a pair of terry-cloth mules, hovered a few inches off the floor as if the dimension between this world and the next occupied a slightly different plane. "I wasn't sure, you see. It's not like I've had any personal experience from this side of the veil, and I thought … well, it doesn't matter what I thought because I was wrong."

Mag's patience lasted long enough for Roma to mutter a few more incoherent, half-finished thoughts, and then she turned to the second ghost. "You. What is your name and why are you here?"

He blinked twice and bought some time to think by taking off his glasses and polishing them on his shirt tail.

"Name's Harold and she"—he indicated Roma with a bob of his head in her direction—"was helping me figure out why I'm still hanging around when I should be lounging on a cloud. I thought she knew what she was doing, but now she's stuck here the same as me. Ironic, isn't it?"

Chapter Three

A snort crawled up the back of Mag's throat, but she swallowed it before it popped out and pissed Roma off. Not that there was much the ghost could do even if she was mad. Tossing around the ectoplasm wasn't likely to impress Mag given the things she'd seen during her lifetime.

"Fine," Roma said. "Tease me if you must, but apparently there's some overlap between Harold's unfinished business and mine. You can wipe that smirk off your face, too. It won't be so funny when you end up with a houseful of permanent guests. Looks like you'll have to help me help them, and then we can all move on together."

"That dog," Jinx said, pointing to the doe-eyed Whizzer, "seems to have a thing for me, and he is not staying here so you're going to do whatever it takes to get rid of him. He's looking at me like I'm his soul mate, or a juicy bone, or something."

Every so often, Jinx showed there was a spine under all the white fur and laziness. His transformation during their vacation at the beach had finally answered Clara's question of how a firecracker like her sister had ended up with such a damp squib of a familiar. There was a tiger in Jinx's tank; he just required a big push to show his stripes.

Then something Roma said clicked in Clara's head. "A houseful of permanent guests?"

Mag sighed. "How many did you bring with you?" She was beginning to think Madame Roselda had known good and well what her gifts were and had had the presence of mind to scamper off before Roma could make her use them.

"Only a few," Roma hedged. "Whizzer should be the worst of them. He's been with me for a month now and I don't have a clue what he needs."

Whizzer deposited another glowing stain on the edge of the hearth. "He *needs* to learn to control his bladder. I assume all of his"—Clara took a second to choose the right word—"essence will go with him when he leaves?"

Roma shrugged.

"Okay, then what's the deal with Harold?" Since he was staring at her with nearly the same look on his face that Whizzer had for Jinx, Clara wanted him gone. Now. Before she had to imagine him watching her while she was sleeping or something.

Roma shrugged again.

Turning to Harold, Clara tried a technique that had worked well for her in the past.

"What's your full name?" She fired off the question, speaking quickly to indicate he should answer in the same way. When he didn't, she snapped her fingers at him. "Don't think about it, just answer quickly." Besides, who had to put that much thought into such an easy question?

"Harold Hardy Loon." Oh, that was why. Clara moved on.

"What did you do for a living?"

"International Data Manager."

"Married?"

"Divorced."

"Favorite movie?"

"Die Hard." What was it with that movie and men?

"What was the name of your first pet?"

"Spinner."

"Were you murdered?"

"No, who would want to kill me? I was the most boring person on the planet. And that's a direct quote from my ex-wife. I fell off a stepladder cleaning the gutters."

She led Harold through a series of questions, making each one more complex as she went, and firing them off rapidly until he answered without thinking. Then she hit him with the money shot.

"What's your unfinished business?"

"I was watching reruns of Dallas and I never got to the part where they said who shot JR."

Even in incorporeal form, Mag would have sworn Harold's cheeks pinked at the admission.

Being the nice person she was, Clara caught the giggle before it escaped and hurt Harold's feelings, and she gave her sister a stern look warning her to do the same. Still, her lips twitched and she had to bite them to make it stop.

"It was Kristin. And she was pregnant with his baby." Dredging that bit of trivia up from her memory, Clara gave him the details.

"Kristin? Huh. I never would have guessed." And with those his parting words, Harold's outline brightened and turned fuzzy.

When the last sparkling mote of him faded into the light, Clara gave in to the fit of laughter she'd been holding back.

"I'm sorry, Roma," she gasped. "I don't mean to make fun of what you do." Tears streaming, Clara's stomach ached, but every time she thought the fit had passed, she remembered the look on Harold's face and started up again.

Used to being the one indulging in inappropriate humor, Mag enjoyed her footing on the high road for once and tried to diffuse by asking Roma, "Does this kind of thing happen a lot?"

"This would be my first television-cliffhanger crossing. You get your old standards: final message for a loved one; the will is in the pages of my favorite book; here's the safe combination. That kind of thing. Then there's the revenge for murder set. Those are my least favorite. They tend to be too aggressive in their demand for restitution. Takes some work to get that type to cross over, but I don't see many murder victims, so that's a mercy."

As if in response to Roma's comment, another tremor ran through the house hard enough to clack Clara's teeth together. Boxes walked to the edges of shelves, and a couple of the smaller ones fell. The tinkling sound of broken glass coming from the shop firmed Mag's mouth into a grim line. A certain amount of breakage was all part of doing business, but this wasn't that.

When the shaking ended, a newly-sobered Clara shot Roma a dirty look and hustled off to check on the state of her shelves.

Roma held up both hands in a gesture of surrender. "Wasn't me. Did you check the history of this place before you moved in?" She tilted her head to one side and drifted toward the door between the workshop and the storefront. What Roma might be listening or sniffing around to find, Mag had no idea.

And that chafed at a woman who was admittedly a control freak when it came to her surroundings. But then, in Mag's former line of work, her life had depended on being aware of the world around her. Going soft now was not in her plan.

"It belonged to our current high priestess, Hagatha Crow, who's at least a thousand years old and one of the most powerful witches I've ever met. Ask five people in town about her past, and you'll get five different answers." Mag explained.

"That leaves a lot of history, even assuming she was part of the mass colonization. I'd imagine she has a good many stories to tell, and so does this house."

Clara thought about what Roma had said, which made her think about the history of the Balefires before her. Hailing from Ireland, her parents had come over on one of the first boats when Mag had been nothing more than a twinkle in her father's eye. Being mortal, her father had passed at the ripe old age of ninety and, their mother shortly thereafter. Tempest Balefire had been a force of nature, and a talented witch, but her heart couldn't bear the loss of her one true love.

She and Mag hadn't exactly been children at the time of their mother's death, and while they'd always known they'd one day lose their father, it hadn't occurred to either of them to prepare for life without Tempest.

Mag had hightailed it, leaving Clara to become the new Keeper of the Flame, a position of authority she held for a good many years until a magical mishap during a fight with her daughter left Clara encased in stone and unable to continue. The baton passed to Clara's granddaughter, Lexi, the current reigning Keeper.

While it had always been painfully obvious to Clara that she'd never learn many of the details of Mag's life on the road, it had only recently begun to occur to *Mag* that she'd left a sizable hole in her sister's existence during the dark years she'd spent running from her grief. It was part of why she'd agreed to move to Harmony in the first place—penance for not being there the last time she'd been needed.

"Hagatha has stories, all right," Mag said, shaking her head. "Problem is, you never know which portions are truth and which portions were whispered by the voices in her head. We're supposed to be keeping her itchy wand hand in check, but most of the time it's like herding butterflies. I doubt she'd choose to be helpful, if I even knew where to find her right now."

The last thing Mag wanted to do was seek Hagatha's assistance, and she wasn't about to admit to Roma that a fraction of the reason had to do with her own pride.

Roma shrugged. "No mind, like I said, you'll help me fix Stephanie's problem and then we'll all be on our way." She looked at Mag expectantly. "Let's go."

"Lead the way, Roma," Mag replied, pride showing in the lines of her jutting chin.

Clara followed as Mag led the way through the shop and out the front door. Roma made it as far as the frame, where from Mag's vantage point on the other side, it looked as if the medium walked into a glass door. Her filmy essence roiled and recoiled back in on itself, and for a moment, there was nothing where the ghost had floated.

Slowly, the frothy white mass reconstituted itself, and bit by bit reformed into the shape of the old medium. She tried again to exit Balms and Bygones, the entire scene playing over once more while Mag and Clara stood, open-mouthed, watching in fascination.

"It looks like you aren't going anywhere, Roma." Mag said gently. She felt little remorse giving her friend a hard time—Mag felt little remorse giving *anyone* a hard time—but she wasn't cold-hearted. Now Roma wasn't simply stuck on this plane of existence. She was stuck in the Balefire house. For how long was anyone's guess.

"And it looks like you're going to have to do some digging, Maggie. Go talk to Stephanie, and then find this Hagatha Crow and figure out what sort of ju-ju she's hexed this place with."

The idea of knocking on some random woman's door made Mag's eye twitch. "What are we supposed to say to this Stephanie? You know she's going to think we're a couple of weirdos, right?"

Grinning at the description, Roma provided enough details that Mag and Clara should be able to convince Stephanie she'd sent them, and then shooed them out the door.

Chapter Four

"I don't care what Roma says, we're going to look crazy if we show up at this woman's door spouting some cockamamie story about a dead medium." Mag seemed worried, an emotion she rarely displayed, giving Clara confirmation of how much she cared about helping Roma find her final peace.

"You've been living in hiding for far too long, Maggie, if you don't remember how effective the truth can sometimes be. Stephanie Huffington is already a believer. I don't think it will be difficult to convince her that we've been sent to help and that our motives are pure. Plus, she's got a little bit of the sight, and from what Roma said, an open and accepting nature."

Clara was unperturbed by the task set before them, and it calmed Mag's nerves enough for her to enjoy the view of town from where they rode, slowly, up Pine Hill toward Huffington Manor.

The VW minibus the Balefires had acquired shortly before moving to the country chugged and clunked as though traveling over potholed dirt, jarring and jostling its passengers even though the road consisted of smooth, meticulously-maintained pavement. One of Mag's little jokes.

Hailing from the fifties, the engine had long since given out, forcing the sisters to resort to magical means to keep it running. In a town like Harmony, where status mattered to many, the Volkswagen was considered an eyesore, a fact that brought a smile to Mag's lips. Any excuse to thumb her nose at the irrelevancies of mortals was icing on her cake.

Though it lacked the pretentiousness to be called such anywhere else, the stately manor considered a mansion by Harmony standards sat in a clearing of white birch and towering pine trees bordered by an intricately wrought iron fence.

Mag half expected an armed guard to greet them at the end of the driveway, but instead found the entrance open and unmanned. Tall pots filled with the last splash of autumn flowers held the gate open in a welcoming gesture. Mag hoped that it was an omen, a foreshadowing of Stephanie's character, and that her sister's reassuring statement would hold true.

Because she valued privacy above all else, the thought of showing up at someone's door with news sure to disturb their equilibrium made Mag twitchy.

As they pulled up in front of the house and climbed out of the VW, it became obvious no expense had been spared to keep Huffington Manor in top condition. A row of perfectly square hedges rose out of a bed of scarlet mulch, and not a speck of the stuff spilled out onto the pristine white walkway.

Autumn had long since chased away the last vestiges of summer heat, but a set of oscillating fans positioned every six feet along the ceiling of a grand wraparound porch carried no trace of dust. There wasn't even a spider web to be found, though the eight-legged freaks guarded the door of every other house in town.

And yet, here and there, it was obvious the owner enjoyed a unique sense of style and humor. A family of garden gnomes with jaunty hats in a rainbow of colors peeked from beneath the hedges. Tendrils of ivy snaked from the top of each stately porch column to kiss the floor with the tips of their leaves.

Mag took a deep breath and shuffled her feet impatiently while Clara tucked a lock of hair behind her ear and jabbed the doorbell.

"Either that door is a good six inches thick or the bell is broken." Mag commented when no jingling or dinging sounded from within. She pressed the bell again and waited, and was just about to start pounding on the door when the latch clicked and a woman wearing an apron slowly pulled it open.

"Hello, how can I help you?" she asked in a matter-of-fact tone with an accent that carried the memory of Yorkshire in its rhythm.

Mag was pleasantly surprised for the second time since finding the gate open when the starched and pressed yet friendly housekeeper motioned for the sisters to follow her inside, accommodating Clara's request to speak to Stephanie without ado.

Chagrined, Mag performed a mental face-palm, realizing she'd just subjected Stephanie Huffington to what she'd spent the last few decades watching her sister endure: judgment without provocation based solely on outward appearance.

In Clara's case, the judgment had come from all of the witches who assumed she'd committed the unpardonable sin of killing another witch—a crime for which the punishment was an eternity turned to stone. When Clara's rocky relationship with her daughter, Sylvana, came to a magical crescendo, leaving Clara frozen mid-spell and Sylvana nowhere to be found, it was assumed the Keeper of the Flame had turned to the dark side and dispatched her own daughter.

Smug and self-righteous, her sisters in magic had paraded in front of her stoned form to confess their own petty crimes to the one person who they knew would never be able to repeat them. It had come as quite a shock when Clara was proved innocent, and upon being restored, it turned out she'd not only heard but remembered each and every indiscretion.

Panic ensued as they expected her to use the information against them.

But those women had been wrong—Clara had more class than they realized, and had kept the secrets of her fellow witches even when it would have behooved her to let them fly from her lips. Amid the aftermath, Mag had vowed to stop making snap judgments, but the practice had become so ingrained it was easy to fall back into old habits. She respected Roma enough to believe Stephanie deserved her best efforts, and reaffirmed her pledge to keep an open mind.

As Clara followed the housekeeper through the foyer, she grew more curious about the woman she was about to meet, but Mag only had eyes for the decor. There was a Demilune console table with a marble top, inlaid marquetry, and exquisitely matched banding detail that sparked a memory from the golden twenties when the piece would have been new.

There'd been a delicious young man and just enough bathtub gin to ensure a good time was had by both. But that was then, and this was now, and she identified with antiques because she felt like one herself most of the time. Old and past her prime.

Except when she and Clara were in the midst of a new mystery and the excitement tingled along her nerves—then she felt alive again. Like right now. This was the beginning of something; she just knew it.

The housekeeper ushered Mag and Clara into the library where a petite blond curled up on a window seat overlooking the golf course-sized backyard. In her arms lay a mottled black, brown, and white mutt of indeterminate breed, the exact opposite type of dog one would expect the richest woman in the county to own.

"Dear, there are some women here to see you."

The little dog hopped down with a thump and wiggled over to the Balefire sisters. He gave each a curious sniff before trotting out along with the housekeeper. His little ears perked and his tail wagged with anticipation when she said something about a treat.

"Thank you, Constance." Stephanie called, then offered a warm, genuine If she felt any irritation or curiosity about receiving unannounced visitors, she didn't let it show. It was a skill likely born from necessity and honed by a lifetime of practice. "I'm Stephanie Huffington. And you are?"

"I'm Clara Balefire, and this is my sister, Margaret." For the first time since moving to Harmony, outside of dealings with the coven, she didn't pretend they were mother and daughter. Stephanie's raised eyebrow indicated her curiosity at how two women who appeared separated in age by at least four decades could be siblings, but maintained her polite composure and didn't press the issue.

"Call me Mag. We've been sent by Roma to lend you our assistance."

Stephanie's hazel eyes widened, and she faltered slightly, "When did you speak to Roma?"

"She visited us last night." Mag explained.

"Well, that's a great story but Roma died last week." Stephanie placed her hands on her hips, fingers trembling even as she returned Mag's steely-eyed gaze. "I attended her funeral."

Mag and Clara exchanged a look, and Clara nodded at her sister. "Go ahead."

"Yes," Mag said, her voice clear, "she did, unfortunately. But that doesn't mean she's gone. And she won't move on until she's sure you're safe. That's why we're here." Listening to the words coming out of her mouth, Mag wouldn't have blamed Stephanie if she booted them to the porch and slammed the door.

But Roma needed help, and Balefire women never turned away a friend, so Mag took a deep breath and prepared to tell Stephanie the truth. The whole truth because Roma thought it was the best way to proceed.

"We're witches, as crazy as that might sound to you. But it's the truth, and Roma thinks you might need our particular brand of help." Pausing, she waited for a response that never came.

Clara jabbed an elbow into Mag's ribs. Telling Stephanie their secret was one thing, but blurting it out with no preamble must have come as a shock. She stepped in to try to soften the blow.

"Roma spoke highly of you and told us about the first time you ever came to visit her. You were six years old, and you couldn't stop staring at a glass unicorn figurine in her curio cabinet. She said you named it Amalthea after the unicorn from "The Last Unicorn" and she found you so charming, she gifted you the figurine."

Pushed out of stasis, Stephanie's expression ran through a gamut of emotions, beginning with incredulity and then softening into acceptance. "I still have Amalthea, and there's no way you could have known about that, so I suppose I have no choice but to believe you."

Still curious, she invited Mag and Clara to sit down on a set of chairs angled toward the breathtaking view. "I can tell that Roma means well, but I don't think it's me who's in danger. I think something might have happened to my fiancé, Bradley. What exactly did she tell you? Wait, first answer one question. Why didn't Roma just come here and communicate to me herself?"

"Well, she wanted to, but it seems she was unable to make contact. Then there were some extenuating circumstances involving our house. We own Balms and Bygones, a little shop on Mystic Street. She came to us for help, and now she's stuck there with the rest of the spirits who followed her through the veil." Clara explained. "I know how it sounds, but I promise you it's real."

The fact that Stephanie didn't bat an eyelash made Mag like her even more. "Balms and Bygones, yes I know the place. And you're those two women who solve murders. I've heard of you." Clearly curious, Stephanie motioned for Clara to continue.

"Roma told us how you'd come to her a few weeks ago, and why. But we'd like to hear the story from your perspective." Clara prompted.

While the girl settled into an armchair, Constance returned to the library carrying a tray of refreshments and offered the Balefires lemonade and cake that looked like it had been made from scratch. She puttered for a moment, straightening a couple of throw pillows and setting a few knick-knacks to rights while her concerned gaze kept returning to Mag and Clara.

"It's okay, Constance, I'm just fine." Stephanie reassured her, "In fact, please take the rest of the afternoon off. I can fend for myself."

Constance sent Clara the type of look a mother gives someone she doesn't quite trust around her child. It was obvious the two enjoyed more than an employer/employee relationship.

"Thank you, Stephanie. There's a homemade macaroni-and-cheese casserole in the refrigerator for you, dear. I think I'll head into town and join the ladies for some Bridge at the senior center. I'll be back this evening." She nodded once at Mag and Clara, then made a hasty retreat.

Stephanie watched the older woman leave, a fond smile curving her lips. "She keeps telling me I'm too thin, and she knows I can't resist her mac and cheese. Constance tends to be protective of me. She was my nanny before she took over managing the house, but she's more like family than an employee." She turned her attention back to Mag and Clara. "Now, let's get back to the business at hand. Poor Roma. I feel responsible. If it weren't for me, she'd be resting in peace."

Mag jumped in to reassure the girl. "I've known Roma since she was a bright-eyed teenager, and never expected her to go quietly into that good night. Communing with the dearly departed piqued her curiosity, and she'd have found some excuse to stick around and see what it's like on the other side of the table. However, I'd prefer if she weren't haunting our shop, especially since she brought an entourage through with her, so let's see what we can do to send her on her way, shall we?"

Stephanie nodded gravely and launched into her tale, "About a year ago, an article about animal kill shelters got under my skin. I made an appointment with a non-profit animal advocacy agency, and expressed an interest in donating to the cause. The director explained that they'd received a sizable grant and enough donations to keep them in the black for the year, but suggested I parcel out the sum to a few of the private rescue shelters that were struggling to stay afloat."

As if her fingers needed something to do, Stephanie used the edge of her fork to cut off a piece of cake, but the bite never made it to her lips.

"I decided to tour the list she gave me, and the first one I went to was run by a man named Bradley Graham. I came home that day with a dog and a date. It was a whirlwind romance, as silly as that phrase sounds. We fell deeply in love, and he proposed six months ago. Everyone said Brad was in it for my money, but they were wrong." Stephanie paused when Mag and Clara exchanged a sideways glance.

Stephanie held up a hand. "I know what you're thinking. People in my situation always say that, but I'm not some silly, air-headed heiress. I went to Yale, for crying out loud. And I can spot a phony from a mile away. Brad encouraged me to do what *I* wanted with my money, and never asked for a penny."

The cake plate made a clinking sound when Stephanie set it back down on the tray.

"He supported my decision to invest in my cousin Cheyenne's business, and even offered to sign a prenup if I wanted one. Does that sound like something someone would do if they were only after my money?"

"Not on the outset, no." Mag was leaning forward, her elbows on the table and her fingers steepled. The cynicism on her face was clear. A con man convincing his mark he was a nice guy while he planned and schemed—oldest trick in the book.

Clara watched Stephanie's face fall. "Don't let my sister get under your skin; she's just cautious and considers every angle. Your financial circumstances have to be considered, even if you're certain money had nothing to do with what happened."

"She's right, I'm a bit of a skeptic," Mag confirmed, "But that doesn't mean you're wrong." She changed the subject, "Roma mentioned you'd been having nightmares. Dreams are full of insights into the inner mind and emotional landscape. Can you tell us about them?"

Stephanie sighed "They started after Brad disappeared, but this isn't my first experience with having nightmares." A wistful expression crossed her face. "After my parents died, I couldn't sleep for months without reliving the crash."

"You were in the car." Clara's heart went out to the girl as Stephanie nodded in answer. "I'm so sorry, dear."

"Yes, well, I've spent a pretty penny on therapy over the years, but it was Roma who finally helped me come to terms with what happened. I believe their souls are at peace, and that's enough for me."

Toying with a heart-shaped locket she wore around her neck, Stephanie took a deep breath, and her eyes fluttered closed for a moment. When they opened, there was sadness and a hint of regret.

"It was just an ordinary day. We were in the car, and I'd wanted to stay home. I was arguing with my mother like any normal 13-year-old. She was annoyed with me, and I wasn't happy with her, either. If I'd known that was my last day with her ..." Stephanie's voice roughened, but she continued.

"My father swerved, but not in time. Now, of course, I realize it wasn't my fault. But every night I relived the experience in my dreams, trying futilely to change the outcome."

"Is that what's happening now?" Clara gently prodded.

"No, this is different. It's dark and I'm alone, I'm scared, and I'm searching for Brad. I can see him walking ahead of me but every time I get close to him, he disappears into the black nothing. I wake up screaming." Stephanie's nose twitched like she was holding back tears, but she maintained her composure.

Mag shifted uncomfortably in her seat. "What do you think happened to him? Why would he be in danger, and from whom?"

"That's just it. I have no idea. He doesn't have any enemies. He's lived over in Woodbridge all his life, he went to State on a full academic scholarship, and he does volunteer work on the weekends. His life is an open book, and none of the pages are smudged. I'm telling you, he wouldn't leave behind everything he'd worked for at the drop of a hat. Not on purpose."

What she left unsaid was as important as her impassioned insistence.

"If Brad had wanted to leave me, he would have been man enough to do it to my face. Everything was fine that night. I fell asleep while he was still working through a stack of paperwork. The next morning he wasn't in bed when I woke up. I figured he'd gone to the shelter early for work, but then I didn't hear from him all day. That evening, I couldn't take it anymore, so I went to his apartment and let myself in. All of his things were gone and there was a note."

Stephanie's forehead wrinkled into a line as her eyes darted back and forth as though she was searching her mind for some hint that would make everything clear. Finding none, she looked to Mag and Clara with sadness and worry written plainly over her face. "But he wouldn't leave me. He just wouldn't. And certainly not like that."

"Did you contact the police or any of his family?" Mag asked.

Stephanie's face contorted for a moment. "Brad doesn't have much family to speak of. We have that in common. Chief Cobb said that since he left a note, he's not missing. And he implied that I might need to see a psychiatrist, since I was having trouble accepting the breakup," she stated bitterly.

Mag snorted. "Chester Cobb is the biggest boob on the planet. Trust me, I know from personal experience."

"You should talk to his deputy, Lynn Nye," Clara suggested. "She's a good cop."

Stephanie dipped her head. "She is. I've known Lynn most of my life. We went to school together. And I already spoke to her. She pretty much agreed with Cobb, though not on the part about the psychiatrist. Lynn said she'd keep her eyes and ears open and contact me if anything turned up. Honestly, I'm not sure how you could possibly help me."

"Don't you worry about that," Mag scoffed. "We're more capable than we look, I promise you. We'll do some digging, and we'll be in touch."

Clara pulled a card emblazoned with the Balms and Bygones logo out of her purse and scribbled something on the back of it before pushing it across the table to the younger woman. "Here's the number to the shop, and my cell is on the back. If you need anything before then, or if anything else comes up, give us a call."

"Thank you, really. I appreciate your concern," Stephanie said, but didn't move from her chair. It seemed like there was something more she wanted to say.

Guessing that was the case, Clara said gently, "You can ask us anything you want, dear." It felt natural to take a motherly role with Stephanie, and she could sense the girl craved the attention.

"What kinds of things can you do? You know, with your witch powers?" she asked bashfully.

A wide smile spread over Mag's face. She took a surreptitious look around and reached out with her witchly senses to make sure nobody but Stephanie would witness what she was about to do. "Now, don't go repeating what you're about to see. Not that anyone would believe it anyway." With that, Mag loosed a bit of Balefire from her finger and set the library fireplace blazing.

Stephanie's face lit up like a kid who caught Santa Claus in the act of scurrying back up the chimney, and promised she'd keep her lips zipped on the subject.

Trailing behind Stephanie toward the front door, Clara watched it open from the outside and her breath caught when a man stepped into the foyer. So strong and powerful and immediate was the attraction, she could have sworn she heard the angels sing.

"Uncle John, I didn't know you were stopping by today." Stephanie enveloped one of the men—there were two, Clara noticed belatedly—in a warm hug, the strained look on her face relaxing a little as she sighed and held on for an extra few seconds of comfort. It was clear she felt completely at ease with her uncle.

The pair of them, she so petite and doll-like with her perfect features and he beaming with pride, made a nice family portrait.

"This is my uncle. John Masters." Stephanie began the introductions.

If Clara had a type—which she didn't, and if she did, she'd never admit it—John Masters ticked every box. Taller than her? Yes, at least six-foot-three given the way he had to bend awkwardly to return his niece's hug. He did so with an ease that showed he'd placed a fair amount of effort into maintaining his physique as time closed the gap between middle age and what comes next.

Even trying not to look too hard, be too obvious, Clara appreciated the way his jacket fell off broad shoulders and the sleeves brushed against hands that looked strong and capable. Romance book covers had it all wrong. Washboard abs were nice, but a strong hand she could imagine trailing fire over her skin—that was sexy. Another box ticked.

An easy smile that went all the way up to spark fire in a set of warm, brown eyes. Tick. Tick. Tick.

Or was that the sound of her heart speeding up?

When he raised his head and those eyes locked on Clara's, they widened just enough to convey shocked pleasure and a sense of recognition even though she knew they'd never met before. She'd have remembered that.

She flipped a lock of burnished sable back over one shoulder with a little head toss that presented the graceful line of her neck to his gaze.

The moment passed when he noticed Mag, and Stephanie explained, "This is Clara and Margaret Balefire, they own a shop in town and were acquainted with Roma."

At the medium's name, John's left eyebrow shot up. The pleasant look slid off his face and he opened his mouth as if to offer an unwanted opinion before choosing to go with a polite, but decidedly cool, "It's nice to meet you."

Stephanie continued the introductions, "And this is Mason Pangborn, an old family friend and our lawyer. He's a partner at Pangborn, McKenzie, and Lowe."

Rosy-cheeked and built like a brick house, the lawyer offered a hearty greeting. His hello carried a false undertone that set off Mag's jackass alarm, and she studied him with suspicion.

Whipping a card out of his pocket, Mason handed it to Clara with a twinkle in his eye, which lingered over her décolletage just long enough to raise her blood pressure a couple of points, and not in the way that his companion had. Now, he was on both the Balefire sister's naughty list. "If you're ever in need of my services …" his emphasis on the word services earned him an eye twitch from Clara and a sharp look from John.

"I'll keep that in mind," Clara commented wryly. "It was nice to meet you." She flashed a dazzling smile at John without thinking and then promised Stephanie they'd be in touch while Mag tried to hold back her opinion of Clara's flirting.

As the door closed, Clara overheard the beginning of their conversation.

Stephanie ask Mr. Pangborn a question. "Do you have the partnership papers I requested for Cheyenne?"

The lawyer's reply was flippant. "Patience, girl. These things take time. We'll work it all out, don't you worry. You've got enough on your mind these days. Any word on what happened to Bradley?"

What sounded like genuine concern threaded through his voice, and Mag and Clara left, hoping Stephanie was in good hands.

Chapter Five

"You were right, Clarie." Mag admitted breathlessly about two seconds after her butt landed in the seat of the van. "That was easier than I thought it would be."

"I would have let you drive, you didn't need to race me to the car." It would be a race against the clock to get home, though, because Mag drove as if someone, somewhere held a checkered flag with her name on it.

The only smart thing to do was hold on and have a few spells at the ready, just in case.

Or distract her with conversation.

"What were your impressions of Stephanie?" Clara prodded.

"I liked her, and I think Roma was right, but that doesn't make me feel any better about the situation. She's a lovely girl, and I'm happy she opened up to us. Problem is, she showed us too many of her cards too quickly. Maybe she's *too* trusting. Maybe her fiancé really is a no-good shyster, and was trying to fleece her for all she's worth."

"If that's true, then it was working, so why would he have left?" Clara fired back. "And furthermore, he's lived nearby his entire life. It's not like he's some grifter with a spotty past. I'm more inclined to believe she's a good judge of character and picked up on our benevolent intentions. Which means she's probably right, and there's something deeper going on there."

Chewing the inside of her lip and driving more slowly than usual, Mag considered what Clara had to say. "Hence the danger Roma mentioned. But if Stephanie happens to be wrong …" she trailed off and took a moment to think. "No, you're right. I can't see what he would stand to gain by leaving. A true shyster would be pushing for a quickie wedding and a trip to the bank to add him to all her accounts."

"Okay, so if we're agreed the fiancé didn't leave willingly, why did he go?"

Lifting a hand off the steering wheel to wave it around, Mag said, "I can think of plenty of reasons. Just for starters, something happened at his work, or there could be another woman. He got in trouble of some kind and now he's on the run."

Clara chided, "You watch too many crime shows on TV."

"At least I didn't know who shot JR." Mag fired right back. "Maybe that uncle of hers is overprotective and paid him off."

"John?"

Mag's eyebrow shot up and she fired a sideways glance at her sister. "Didn't know you were on a first name basis already."

Clara scowled. "Shut up, Maggie. And don't start harping about my love life."

"You don't have one." Mag pointed out. "So there's nothing to harp about. Except you can't deny there were sparks between you. The air practically sizzled when you locked eyes with him."

"Let it go, please."

"Whatever you say." The careful lack of snark and easy agreement didn't fool Clara one iota. The stubbornest of mules could learn a few tricks from Margaret Balefire when she had her teeth into something, and the sweeter she seemed, the more she needed watching.

That was why, when Clara spied the stooped figure of Hagatha Crow stomping through the grass along the side of the road, relief outweighed annoyance. At least there would be no more discussion of men.

Mag slowed down and prepared to stop. "Wonder what she's doing way out here. She looks mad. I think we'd better see if she needs a ride."

Quite possibly the oldest living witch in the world, Hagatha was a regular fixture in the town of Harmony. Until recently, she'd been the head of the Order of the Moonstones, the civic organization she'd formed to hide regular coven meetings from a town full of non-magical people.

"You know there's no reason for her to be walking unless she wants to." Clara referred to a witch's ability to skim between places in the blink of an eye, but reached for the window roller anyway. "But I suppose you're right; we should check. She's been suspiciously quiet since we put an end to the pixie invasion, and it looks like rain."

"Hello Hagatha," she said when Mag pulled up alongside. "Do you want a lift back to town?"

Hagatha's face might have looked like an apple left to wrinkle in the sun, but mischief glittered in her beady eyes. "Penelope Starr sending her watchdogs after me again?"

"What?" Clara said, suspicion in her voice. "No. Was there a reason she should? You're not up to no good, are you?" Not that asking would garner anything close to a straight answer out of old Haggie.

"Hop in, it's warm in here and the day's turning chilly." Mag offered.

Hagatha climbed into the back seat with a concerted effort. She held the collars of her tweed jacket together at her neck and shivered. "Snow's coming early this year. My knee is screaming and that always means snow."

"It isn't even November yet." Clara raised an eyebrow, hoping old Haggie's bum knee was just reacting to too much walking.

Hagatha shrugged. "You can't tell me that in over two hundred years, you've never seen an early squall? Don't you remember the year without a summer? 1816, I believe."

Clara did, indeed, remember that summer, when nobody understood why Jack Frost was still out and about in July. "Well, nowadays we'd know if there was a volcanic eruption on some distant part of the earth affecting weather patterns."

"It's funny to me that a witch of Balefire caliber would believe that ridiculous explanation." Hagatha commented, refusing to say another word on the subject.

It took only a sideways flick of her eye to draw on enough magic to pop open the back door so Hagatha could stow her tennis ball-footed walker in the cargo space. "Penelope was born in a tizzy, and whatever one she's in now has nothing to do with me."

Snorting quietly, Mag checked for traffic and pulled back onto the blacktop. "I can see that right enough. She's turned twisted knickers into her own private fashion statement, but you can't deny you enjoy tossing her into the spin cycle just for fun."

Hagatha cackled, her eyes alight with humor. "Gives me something to do while I wait to die."

"Say, Hagatha," Mag ventured when the minibus had been silent for a solid three minutes. "Is there anything we ought to know about your old house?"

"Probably several things, Margaret, but I'm going to need more information." Hagatha snuggled deeper into her coat as if the snow she'd predicted had already begun to fall, and Clara turned the heat up another notch.

Mag sighed and explained what had happened with Roma and the other spirits.

"It probably just needs a good cleansing." Hagatha stated without giving any other helpful information. "Stop right here, I'll walk the rest of the way."

"But Romilda's place is just up there," Mag protested.

"Yes, I know that. I'm not senile." Hagatha spat back but offered no reason for wanting to be dropped off a stone's throw from her destination. "Don't you two forget about the full moon celebration Friday night. Wouldn't want to disappoint the children, now, would you?"

With a reassurance that they'd be in Dawkin's woods at dusk the next night, and against her better judgment, Mag let Hagatha out on the side of the road. Clara watched as she dismounted less than gracefully, and kept her eyes trained on the old witch's retreating form while her sister pulled away. So quickly Clara wasn't quite sure she was seeing what she thought she was seeing, a tiny honey pixie poked her head out above Hagatha's tweed collar and then burrowed back inside after casting a wink in Clara's direction.

She opened her mouth to relay the information to Mag, and then closed it again. Mag had been an integral part of the plan to get rid of the Faeland-hailing pixies after the rainforest habitat Hagatha had created for them threatened a drought that would have effectively canceled the town's annual canoe race—and any chance for a successful harvest season.

But, Mag had also harbored a soft spot for Maypole, the pixie who had just winked at Clara like a kid with her hand in the cookie jar. The pixie who had *not* gone back to Faeland with all of her friends as they'd thought.

Back at Balms and Bygones, Clara paced the floor in front of the parlor fireplace while Mag warmed her toes in the Balefire. Roma hovered around, blinking in and out and causing the lamps to flicker incessantly.

"Can't you stop that?" Mag barked harsher than she'd intended. She preferred the quiet solitude of her backyard hut on a good day, and having a ghost hovering over her—old friend or not—constituted anything but a good day. It was grating on her nerves.

"Solve the mystery and I'll have somewhere else to go," Roma replied, kicking her antics up a notch while Whizzer romped about excitedly.

A mighty crash sounded from above, and Clara about jumped out of her skin. "Pyewacket?" she hollered. "What's going on up there?" Clara hoped nothing in her bedroom had been broken, and rushed upstairs just as Pye exited the room with an irritated expression on her face.

"Everything is fine, except for the fact that my nap was interrupted by another damnable ghost. She's gone now." Pye fixed Clara with a self-satisfied stare.

"How did you get her to go away?" Clara asked, curiosity obliterating her irritation.

Pye's lips curled into a decidedly feline smile. "I used your cell phone to pull up her Facebook account.

She moved on once she realized her boyfriend had received her last text message. They'd had a fight, and she couldn't go into the light thinking he might not have seen her apology. Not that it makes any difference, in my humble opinion."

Clara rolled her eyes and bounded back down the stairs with a thump. "Crisis averted. Too bad they aren't all that simple. Though, that does give me an idea." She disappeared into the shop and returned a few moments later with her laptop.

"How is that going to help us?" Mag's question lacked its usual disdain for modern technology. Clara's methods had proven invaluable in the past, much as Mag hated to admit it.

Clara shot her sister an exasperated look. "You really have no idea what's happening on the Internet, do you?"

"No, I don't, and you know it. And I don't care, so what's your point?"

"People post everything from what they had for breakfast to where they're going on vacation to their kids' shoe sizes. But more importantly, they post photos and tidbits of information that might be useful in tracking someone down. Basically, we're going to cyber-stalk Brad." Clara booted up the computer and avoided making eye contact with Mag, who finally relented and agreed to peruse Facebook with an open mind.

"Here we go. Bradley Graham, thirty years old, in a relationship with Stephanie Huffington. That's him all right." Clara clicked on Brad's profile picture and scrolled through his recent photos, noting how besotted he appeared in all the ones including Stephanie.

Mag pointed at the screen. "The last time he posted was the day before he left, is that correct?"

Clara made sure the feed showed recent posts first and nodded. "Yep, it sure is. That tracks with the time of his disappearance. Look at most of these—they're either about Stephanie or about work. He was dedicated, just like she said. Doesn't add up to him packing up and leaving."

"Well," Mag drew out the word in a skeptical tone. "There's no evidence he didn't. Probably got cold feet. A woman like that comes with baggage; it might have been too much for him to take on." She chanced a look at Roma, whose eyes had narrowed to slits.

"I didn't come to you so you could drag poor Stephanie's name through the mud." Roma snapped, her edges blurring.

Mag gave it right back to her. "No, you came to me because you didn't have any other choice."

She stopped talking abruptly as a wintry wind blew through the parlor, calling all the hairs on her arm to attention.

"Stephanie Huffington's baggage is none of your concern!" Roma wailed. "Margaret Balefire, don't make me make you sorry—"

"Make me sorry for what, Roma? I'm already sorry you came here and got me all entangled in your unfinished business. But you asked for my help and now you're all ticked off because the outcome isn't what you expected!" Mag fired back.

The temperature in the room dropped a few more degrees as the ghostly witch slammed her hand on her hip and wagged a finger at the sisters.

"You listen to me, because I'm only going to say this once: I'm not leaving here until you help Stephanie and figure out what happened to Bradley Graham. The man did not just up and disappear into thin air, and I won't be satisfied until you find him. If you don't want me and half of the undead contingency of Harmony camping out in your living room for the next hundred years, you'd better hop on your broomstick and work that Balefire magic." The house rumbled beneath where her feet hovered above the floor while Roma crossed her arms and squared off against Mag, who turned beet red and looked like she was about to shoot steam out of her ears.

Half horrified and half amused, Clara sat back, her mouth agape. Yeah, she'd definitely missed out at not having met the living incarnation of Roma.

"I said we'd help and I don't break promises, Roma." Mag turned away and refused to acknowledge the ghost after her parting shot. "Now shut your yap and let us do what we do."

Chapter Six

"I thought Sundays were supposed to be for relaxing. This does not qualify," Mag commented, wiping a coating of soil off her hands and onto the front of her raspberry-colored tunic. Clara winced, having bought the garment for her sister as an alternative to the 1970s remnants Mag typically wore. Apparently, the absence of outdated paisley prints and tie-dyed colors had relegated Clara's gift to yard work-appropriate attire.

"You know as well as I do that Mother Nature doesn't care what day it is," Clara reminded her sister. "If we don't get all these beds prepared for winter, we'll be looking at a significant amount of spell work to make it right next spring. Especially if old Haggie's knee is accurate and we're going to get an early frost. I'd really rather not take the chance on Mrs. Green seeing anything magical from her post by her kitchen window, and I doubt she'll have deserted it by the time the snow melts."

Mag grinned, and bent back over to continue her task, taking care to settle her leg into the most comfortable position possible. "That woman needs to get a new hobby." She spread a layer of compost onto the square of garden patch at her feet, admiring the way

Clara had arranged the beds both horizontally and vertically to maximize space and create shady corners for plants that required less sun.

"The only time she leaves her house is for knitting group and the garden and book clubs. But I don't think her motives have much to do with keeping anything but her big mouth busy. Though, as far as neighbors go, she could be worse. That hummingbird cake she brought over last month was delicious." Clara's mouth watered at the thought of the moist, walnut-studded loaf coated in a thick layer of cream-cheese frosting.

Idly, Clara made a mental note that between Evelyn's donuts, the snacks offered at every community gathering, and the plates of goodies regularly dropped off by friendly neighbors, she'd be quite a few pounds heavier come spring if she didn't rein it in. Witch genetics might keep her looking young, but they had no effect whatsoever when it came to net calories.

Mag had long ago decided that since she already looked as though she was entering her crone phase of life, it didn't matter much whether she had a little extra junk in her trunk. The idea of counting calories seemed about as useful to her as a screen door on a submarine, and nothing was worth giving up her butter pecan ice cream addiction.

"Clara, can you please come inside and pick up your phone?" Pyewacket hollered from the back porch in an irritated tone, interrupting the serenity her companion had been enjoying. "It's been ringing for a solid ten minutes and this is my day off. Between the random ghosts, the customers, and the phone, this place is entirely too loud lately." She arched one perfectly-shaped eyebrow and retreated back indoors, presumably to grapple with Jinx over the coveted spot next to the roaring Balefire.

Clara hurried inside, Mag on her heels, and picked up her cell phone from the counter in the back room of the shop where she'd left it. Before she had a chance to look at the screen, Roma appeared out of the ether and spewed in a frustrated tone, "Stephanie Huffington has called six times while you ladies were out playing in the dirt."

"That can't be good." Clara's eyebrows furrowed as she contemplated the implications.

"Call her back already." Roma demanded, earning herself a sideways glance from Mag, whose patience was stretched to the breaking point when it came to the ghost of her dear friend.

Or perhaps, Clara thought, this was the kind of relationship they'd always had—the kind of relationship Mag had with most of the people she knew. Anyone who had hung around long enough to learn how big her sister's heart was also knew she was mostly bluster, and Roma appeared unperturbed by Mag's gruff demeanor. It earned her a few more points in Clara's book.

"Hello?" Stephanie's voice was strained and hoarse when she answered the phone, and Clara could tell she'd been crying.

"Hi Stephanie, are you all right?" Motherly concern threaded through Clara's tone.

Stephanie blurted, "No, I'm not, and I'm sorry for bothering you and I didn't know who else to call, but you said Roma sent you to help. Something has happened. I'm not sure exactly what's going on, but would you and your sister mind coming by today? As soon as possible, if it's not too much trouble."

Mag, her head bent over Clara's, noticed how even in the throes of whatever had prompted her to call two virtual strangers for assistance, Stephanie still maintained a level of politeness Mag wouldn't have attempted even on her best day.

"Of course. We'll head right over. Are you safe?" Clara asked, though she expected so, or presumably, Stephanie would have called the police regardless of her feelings about Chief Cobb.

Stephanie assured her she was in no physical danger, and Clara disconnected the call with another promise to hurry.

Stephanie answered the door before either Mag or Clara could ring the bell, and though her hair had been smoothed into a neat topknot and she was fully dressed, it was clear from the red rings around her eyes that the previous night's sleep hadn't been a restful one.

"Thank you so much for coming." Cold fingers closed over Clara's warm ones and drew her inside. Mag followed.

"I know I must seem like a raving lunatic, and I'll give you fair warning: that might actually be the case."

She ushered the sisters through a Food Network-worthy kitchen bathed in shades of yellow and into a lavish but homey sitting room positioned on the southern side of the house.

Through a set of bay windows, Clara could make out the edges of an impressive herb garden. Even though it was wildly inappropriate given the circumstances, she vehemently hoped the opportunity to view more of the house and grounds would arise.

Under normal circumstances, Mag would have been thinking the exact same thing, her antiquer's eye roving the space for rare and interesting finds. But she once again found herself in the all-too familiar situation of being counted on to provide assistance to someone either more unfortunate than she, or less able to help themselves. In other words, her comfort zone.

"Can I offer you anything to drink?" Stephanie clung to conventions of politeness in the same way she would have clutched onto a life raft, but Clara noticed her hands were shaking.

"No, thank you. We're fine."

Once her guests were seated and she was assured of their comfort, Stephanie settled onto the opposite end of the sofa from Clara. As soon as her back touched the floral brocade, her put-together facade crumpled like a sheet of tissue paper, and though her throat worked with the effort to hold them back, she finally burst into tears.

"What is it, dear?" Mag prompted gently while Clara moved to gather the girl into her arms and make soothing sounds. Sometimes Clara wondered if her sister saved all her patience for other people, and had none left to spare for herself. Mag might have argued that that's how it should be.

After a minute or two, Stephanie gathered herself together and launched into her story.

"It's all a mess, and I'm starting to think Cobb is right and I need to go check myself into a facility. The last two days, I keep finding things out of place. I expect that in the common spaces since there are other people living here, but not in my personal areas. My office, my bedroom."

"Who has access?" Mag asked.

"I don't lock my bedroom door, but the office is always locked. Brad had a key, and Constance has a master that works on every lock in the house. No one else can get in there. Maybe I'm just imagining things because I'm not sleeping well, which is the other reason I called you here."

"Ever since Brad … well, I told you I've been having nightmares and now they're getting worse. The one last night was so vivid it was like a movie playing in my head. Except I was in the movie, not watching it." She shivered, and snuggled into the nubby chenille throw Clara took from the back of an armchair and draped across her shoulders.

"I remember Brad and I were fighting, which isn't something we've ever done. Don't get me wrong— we've had our moments of irritation just like anyone else. But I know exactly how fast your family can be taken away. None of the petty life stuff means anything compared to that."

From the greatest tragedies come the greatest lessons, but if Clara could turn have turned back time for Stephanie, she'd have done it and never counted the cost.

"Besides," the younger woman continued, "Brad is the most even-keeled person I've ever met. We talk through our issues like adults. Except not in my dream. It felt so real, but at the same time muddled, you know? Like I couldn't hear my own words, only what Brad was saying. He was talking about money."

Stephanie paused, and during the silence her eyes darted back and forth, making Mag wish she could just crawl into the poor girl's head and see what it was she was seeing.

She let the money comment slide by, but that didn't mean she hadn't made a mental note of it. Stephanie might not understand that even the most seemingly rational person could turn greedy when finances became involved. It wasn't her fault; she'd never been strapped for cash and had no idea what kind of toll it could take on a person.

"I know it's hard to explain," Mag said. "Dreams always are. You dream with all five senses, but when you recount them it's all about the visual."

"Exactly," Stephanie confirmed. "What I saw and what I felt don't fit together because I was inside Brad's perspective for part of it."

Clara opened her mouth to ask the burning question, but was quelled by a look from her sister.

"He was furious, but underneath the anger, he felt like he'd been betrayed. It was like a fist in the gut." Another sob escaped and Stephanie had to force herself to say the rest.

"His eyes. They were full of hate and I could feel them cutting into me like knives. He turned away and I saw myself grabbing a glass paperweight from the desk and whacking him over the head with it. That's when I woke up." Stephanie looked absolutely miserable as she finished recounting the dream.

Mag stepped in before Clara had a chance to open her mouth, but expressed the same sentiment her sister was about to voice. "It was just a dream. You know that, right?"

"But I—" Stephanie was interrupted by a clink coming from the hallway, and then by Constance wheeling in a cart with an antique porcelain tea service into the room. She ignored the palpable tension and began filling rose-decorated cups with water from the pot. "I thought you could use a cuppa, dear. I've brought a selection of flavors and some fresh-baked muffins. You need to eat."

"Thank you, Constance," Stephanie said. "I promise I'll have a bite." She waited until the door had shut behind the woman before returning her attention to Mag and Clara. "Constance thinks everything can be solved by a cup of tea. But she just doesn't understand."

"Understand what?" Clara asked. "It's okay, you can tell us."

"It felt more like a memory than a dream. I think Brad is dead." Stephanie stared down at her fingers, twisting the blanket between them for a moment that stretched out long. When she looked up, her eyes were filled with conviction. "And I'm almost certain I killed him."

"That's crazy," Mag exclaimed before she had time to think.

"I did warn you." Strangely calm now that she'd made her confession, Stephanie sucked in a breath and let it out in a long sigh. "It feels like I can remember doing it, only it's all hazy. What else could have happened?"

Mag and Clara exchanged a silent conversation of a look. Subtle eyebrow movements and twists of lips spoke volumes, and when it was done, Mag took point in a matter of fact tone.

"A hundred things could have happened and none of them would involve you killing your fiancé. Now, tell us the dream again. From the beginning, and don't leave anything out."

Calmer now, Stephanie repeated the story, and when she was done, Mag asked her to lean back, close her eyes, and picture the beginning of the dream.

"Pause it right at the beginning and tell me where you're at. What can you see?"

Straining to follow Mag's commands, Stephanie's shoulder muscles bunched. "Just Brad's face, like before. Everything else is hazy the way it is when you look outside on a rainy day and the window is foggy and wet."

Another look passed from Mag to Clara, who pitched her voice low and soothing. "Just breathe into it. Let the tension drip down your body and flow into the ground."

It took several minutes of encouragement before Stephanie finally let go and sighed into a more relaxed posture.

"What is Brad saying?" Mag took over again.

"I can't … he looks so angry … something about money and books." Her voice dropped an octave as she imitated a lower pitch. "Where's the other set of books?"

Now, they were on to something. Mag's stomach jumped twice and then settled to a soft flutter. The same way it always had when she was closing in on her prey. "Keep going. Tell me what you hear."

Stephanie's eyelids fluttered while she accessed the memory. "The bang of his fists on the table." A short pause. "No, the desk. He is pounding on the desk. I can hear my own breath wheezing in and out. My heart is beating fast and my face feels hot."

Speaking softly to keep Stephanie from dropping out of the meditative state, Mag probed, "Yours or Brad's?"

"I don't know; it's all running together. I feel like I'm in both skins."

"Describe the desk." The gentle request came from Clara, who thought focusing on something mundane would provide a little breathing room from the escalating emotions.

"Looks like mission oak. Brad turning away. I can see the back of his head, and I don't want to do it, but I can see myself pick up the paperweight."

"What does it look like?"

"Round with colored swirls. The glass is cold and smooth and hard."

With a cry, Stephanie bolted up off the couch, her eyes wild and her breath panting, her hand going to the back of her head and clutching. "I killed him. I can feel the blood on my hands." She collapsed into Clara's waiting arms.

"Way to go, Maggie. She's fainted." Even as she shot a dirty look her sister's way, Clara went into first aid mode and lowered Stephanie to the sofa as gently as she could, given the girl had gone all dead weight. "We need to get her feet elevated. That was just cruel."

In the act of shoving a pillow under Stephanie's feet, Mag replied coolly, "You think so? I think I just did her a huge favor."

"How do you figure?" Clara dipped a napkin in one of the glasses of ice water on the cart and applied the cool cloth to the younger woman's chalk-white forehead.

"I made her give me some evidence to track. The desk and the paperweight." Mag had apparently forgotten it was Clara who had brought up the desk, but she let it slide. No use getting into an argument when there were more important things to worry about.

"You think it's possible that what she dreamed actually happened." It was more a statement than a question, and a good one at that. Stranger things had certainly happened, and they couldn't afford to discount any possibility.

"We'll do a room-by-room search, and if we find them, we'll see if we can turn up a few more clues. Roma said she had a touch of the sight. It could be coming out in these dreams, but we only have Roma's word on that, so we'll look for proof and settle the matter one way or another."

As plans went, it wasn't the worst one Clara had ever heard, but with her sympathies still engaged, she wasn't about to admit that to Mag. Chafing Stephanie's chilled fingers to warm them, she looked at her sister. "Do you think she killed him?"

"I hope not," was the terse response. "Hush now, she's coming around."

When Stephanie's eyes fluttered open, they were haunted and sparkled with tears. "Call the police," she whispered. "I need to turn myself in."

"Not just yet." Mag patted her shoulder in an awkward attempt to soothe her. This wasn't her area of expertise. But sleuthing was. "Let us call Constance to sit with you. Give us permission to take a look around before you go making any rash decisions based off what might have been nothing more than a dream."

Taking a softer approach, Clara pushed gently, "You called us to help and that's all we want to do. Give us an hour or two, please."

After a moment, Stephanie nodded.

Mag got down to business.

Chapter Seven

While Clara sat with Stephanie, Mag bearded Constance in her den. Okay, so calling an immaculate kitchen a den might be a stretch, but that was where she found the housekeeper polishing silver with a vengeance. She looked up when Mag limped into the room and her expression was guarded.

"Mind if I ask you a few questions about the night Brad disappeared?" Sometimes, even when she tried her best, Mag missed a pleasant tone and landed somewhere between brusque and aggressive.

This was one of those times, but Constance wasn't having it. She fixed Mag with a mama bear of a look and said, "She's not going to give you money."

The comment flustered Mag, something that didn't happen all that often and threw her off her stride. "I … what?"

"I won't have it. Whatever woo-woo game you've cooked up, you can quit it now. She's not going to pay you a red cent."

Sucking a breath in through her nose and letting it out the same way, Mag called on every shred of patience she could muster. "Look, I know there are plenty of grifters out there and you've probably dealt with more than your fair share, but we're not after Stephanie's money."

Constance waved the butter knife she'd been polishing and Mag couldn't help but assess the silver's age and try to place the maker by the pattern. It was second nature to her by now.

Catching the look, Constance crowed, "See, there's that look again. You're just as greedy as the rest of them. I saw it all over you the first day you showed up here to gawk at the place and you're almost drooling right now."

Unable to help herself, Mag grinned. "You're right. I can't help myself when I see beautiful old things still being used. Antiques are a passion for me and my fingers itch to touch them. I am greedy, but only to know who made that knife. And to imagine how happy the smith would have been to know his work had lasted all this time."

A grunt of disbelief and a raised eyebrow from Constance made Mag continue and this time it was her eyes that fired.

"I wouldn't take the knife if you offered it to me. Not for free. We Balefires pay our own way. Always. Now, I'm going to help Stephanie by getting to the bottom of what happened here the night Brad disappeared. Not for money, but because a friend asked me for a favor."

Favor didn't exactly describe being held hostage by ghosts, but it was the best explanation Mag planned to give.

Cooler now, Mag leveled Constance with a direct look. "Believe me or not, that's your choice, but we are going do everything in our power to get to the bottom of this, with or without your approval. If you want to help Stephanie, tell me what you remember about the last night Brad spent in this house."

Silence fell around a Clint Eastwood-worthy face-off.

Constance flinched first. She tossed out her earlier statement again as both a reiteration and a warning. "She's not paying you." And then unbent enough to tell her story. Which, as it turned out, wasn't much of one anyway.

"I've been over and over it in my head, and I can't think of anything special or different about that night. Brad is a good man and he loved my girl for her, not her money. He lost his breath every time she walked into the room. You can't fake that kind of thing."

Mag would beg to differ, but she'd barely managed to get on the edge of Constance's good side, so she kept her doubts to herself.

"Nothing stands out at all?"

Laying the shining knife back on the table, Constance waved Mag to a seat and set about what she'd shown to be her go-to in times of stress, putting on another pot of tea.

Impatient to be on with her business, Mag opened her mouth to protest, then shut it again when a plate of macarons landed in front of her in all their delicate pastel glory. She'd have preferred milk to tea, but the cookies were a particular favorite of hers.

Even better, as she settled back in her seat, Constance pushed the velvet-lined tray of silver over to allow Mag a chance to choose a piece and look at the hallmark. It might have been only a delaying tactic, but if it was, it was effective.

"We had salmon for dinner that night. And yes, I say we. Over the years, the lines have blurred, and I like to think I have her mother's blessing for treating Stephanie like one of my own. We're family to each other."

Nodding, Mag nipped off another bite of macaron, and waited for Constance to continue.

"There's nothing much else to tell. After dinner, I went home and watched my stories."

And finally, a tidbit Mag could use.

"Went home? I thought you lived here."

"Oh, I do. Newly married couples need their privacy, and to be honest, I like a bit of my own. When Brad proposed, I thought it was high time I found my own place. Newly married couples need their privacy," Constance repeated, insistent. "Not that *some people* have the same consideration, but Stephanie wouldn't have it. I'm approaching retirement age, and she's got it in her head it's time she took care of me instead of the other way around."

The sharp scent of polish and the swish of cloth over silver continued and so did Constance.

"Next thing I know, she's hired a contractor and an architect to convert some space and add on a little. I have my own little home, but it's still connected to the house."

"So you were on the spot, so to speak, but not within hearing distance that night?"

Constance nodded. "Yes, that's right. My hearing isn't what it used to be, regardless. But I can tell you I came in to make Stephanie a cup of herbal tea at around ten o'clock, and everything seemed fine. Then, in the morning, he was gone without a trace."

Mag ran that information around in her head for a minute before picking up on the one odd thing Constance had said. "You mentioned that some people had no consideration for Stephanie's privacy. What did you mean?"

Constance yanked the tray of silver back over, grabbed a serving spoon, and started polishing like she wanted to get to the chewy, Tootsie-Roll center. "Cheyenne," she said, as if Mag ought to know already.

"She was supposed to stay here —crash is the word she uses—for a couple of weeks before classes started. Then she met that juvenile-delinquent boyfriend of hers at a coffee shop. Calls himself a brew steward. What is that supposed to mean, I ask you?"

"Kids these days," Mag said because it seemed to be the expected response. "Cheyenne is Stephanie's cousin, right?"

"Yes, but she's not a Huffington." Constance declared, as if that made any difference when it came to family. "Cheyenne comes down from her mother's side. Feckless idiot, if you ask me, but Stephanie wouldn't turn her away, so in she moved and then up and transfers schools to be closer to that coffee-making twit."

Tell me how you really feel, Mag thought, but kept that to herself. "Was Cheyenne here that night?"

"Not that I saw. Sleeps over at her boyfriend's house most nights, but she keeps odd hours studying and working. On her last year of business school and already thinks she's capable of running one herself. Might be, too, if she'd focus less on that good-for-nothing she's attached herself to. If you want to know where Cheyenne was that night, you can ask her yourself. I saw her slink in here not an hour ago."

Other than giving Mag another line to tug, Constance hadn't been a lot of help. "Could you come sit with Stephanie while we take a look around?" And because she could see the other woman gearing up to protest, she added, "You can check our pockets before we leave if it makes you feel any better."

"Don't think I won't." But Constance followed Mag willingly.

"I feel so violated," Mag muttered.

She very nearly was when Constance got a look at Stephanie's pale face and tear-ravaged eyes. If dirty looks could break skin, both the Balefires might have exploded on the spot.

Mag and Clara left the pair in the sitting room and made their way throughout the rest of the house. The main floor boasted high, coffered ceilings and intricate moldings that would have given the rooms a more formal feel if not for the use of cheerful fabrics in bold colors and patterns.

Framed family photos hung side by side with paintings that might well have belonged in a museum. Clara found the juxtaposition charming and considered the placement as physical evidence of how Stephanie valued people over things.

Even if they found a bloody paperweight under her pillow, Clara would have a hard time believing a woman like that would kill her fiancé over money. It just did not compute. "I don't think she did it."

"I think sometimes you let your emotions get the best of you." Mag retorted. "It's better to remain vigilant, and open to any possibility. If she *did* do it—and mind you, I'm not saying I'm sold on the idea either—then this could be the danger Roma sensed."

Clara sighed, "Fine, let's keep moving, then. We've seen every room on the first floor and there's no desk here like the one Stephanie described."

"No, but it *was* a dream," Mag allowed, "and she said she couldn't get a good handle on her surroundings. I'm more concerned about the paperweight."

"You don't think she'd know if she owned a paperweight of that description?" Clara asked.

Mag shrugged, "She never said she didn't. This house is enormous, and she's not the only one who lives here. I think we'd be negligent if we didn't take a look around and see if there's anything that appears out of place. Think about it—you bash someone over the head, there's bound to be evidence. And how would she have gotten the body out of the house by herself?"

Looking at it that way, Clara realized Mag was looking to rule out rather than to prove.

"I can't see her having the ability to pull off something like that on her own, and then only remember it in a dream. Another reason why it seems unlikely she played a role. But you're right; we've got to check all the angles. We're most likely looking at a case of creative denial and a keen imagination. But, I can't say I'm willing to pass up the chance to nose around this place," Clara admitted. And, there it was.

Mag grinned and nodded, then circled back to the front entrance where a grand pair of staircases arced up to a second-floor balcony, branching off into two wings. From what Stephanie had said, her suite was positioned to the left and her cousin Cheyenne's to the right, with a row of guest rooms separating the two.

A thorough search of Stephanie's bedroom proved nothing more than the girl's love of all things pink, and there was no desk or paperweight of the type described, even in the locked office adjacent to her sleeping quarters. The guest rooms netted a similar result, and with no other place to search, Mag and Clara found themselves standing in front of the mysterious Cheyenne's closed door bickering over what to do next.

"We can't just barge in. Constance said she was home." Mag hissed.

"Then just knock on the door." Clara whispered back.

"No, you."

"No—never mind," Clara rolled her eyes and decided engaging in a childish argument with her sister, no matter how tempting, wouldn't help matters. She raised a hand and knocked lightly on the door.

When no one answered, Clara put her ear to the door and tuned into her witchy senses. "There's nobody in there. Let's just have a peek."

"You're a regular rebel, Clara Balefire." Mag said with a mixture of mockery and genuine admiration.

Clara creaked the door slowly open and took in the scene before her. A large four-poster bed sat on a platform in one corner, the covers rumpled and pillows tossed haphazardly over the floor. Every surface was covered with articles of clothing—many still carrying the store tags—bottles of expensive hair and skincare products, and enough half-empty glasses to stock one of Mag's hutches at Balms and Bygones. In short, the room was a mess, and it was clear that Constance had chosen to leave Cheyenne to her own devices.

Mag let out a low whistle. "It's taking everything I have inside not to let loose a cleaning spell over this room. How can people live like this? And what on god's green earth are these?" Mag held up a g-string thong and wrinkled her nose at it.

"Trust me, you don't even want to know," Clara said, attempting to hold back a giggle.

"You're probably right about that. Regardless, I don't think we're going to find what we're looking for poking around in here. Let's check outside." Knowing full well they wouldn't find what they were looking for outside, Mag avoided Clara's gaze and took advantage of the opportunity to snoop even further.

"A house this size might look like a fortress, but there must be half a dozen ways to get in or out. You've got your second floor balconies. Notorious for being left unlocked because people assume height equals security. Rookie mistake." Mag exited through an unlocked side door and pointed upward. Using the tip of her cane to sweep away newly fallen leaves, she inspected the ground for disturbances.

"This area's clear." Satisfied, she continued her sweep of the exterior of Stephanie's home. "Let's check the backyard."

Clara fell into step beside her sister, thrilled to finally get the chance to check out the grounds, and meandered through what felt like an old English garden with a modern twist. This late in the fall, all that was left were the hardier plantings—shrubs and some ornamental grasses, but come spring, it would be a showplace.

After rounding another curve in the garden path, Clara's breath caught in her throat and Mag stopped dead in her tracks when what looked like an authentic gypsy wagon loomed into view. Pretty painted flowers traced along the faded green body of the wagon and along the trim around windows and door. The domed top created a cheery arch against the sky.

The biggest surprise was finding their host there.

Stephanie leaned on one arm against the wagon's porch rail, talking to a girl of about twenty-two who sat on the steps with her elbows on her knees. When she caught sight of Mag and Clara approaching, she waved them over with a weary hand. It seemed her time spent with Constance had been bracing because the blotchy redness around Stephanie's eyes had receded dramatically. Or maybe the housekeeper was right and a good cup of tea was all she'd needed.

"This is my cousin, Cheyenne. Cheyenne, meet my new friends, Clara, and her—"

Catching Stephanie's eye, Clara emphasized, "My mother, Mag Balefire."

Both sisters noted that Stephanie hadn't mentioned the real reason for their presence. "Chey works out here sometimes. Says the patterns give her inspiration."

"It's very nice to meet you." Clara extended a hand while Mag simply nodded and kept her eyes peeled. She had her suspicions about Stephanie's cousin, and the state of her suite upstairs hadn't improved Mag's opinion.

Knowing Clara would reprimand her for passing judgment, she decided she didn't much care. She'd trust her intuition, thank you very much, and if Cheyenne did something to change her mind, she'd happily admit she'd been wrong. Well, maybe happily wasn't the right word—grudgingly might be more appropriate, if Mag were being honest. Old habits died hard, but she'd admit it.

Cheyenne stood up and grasped Clara's hand warmly. "Nice to meet ya," the girl drawled in a thick southern accent. However, this was no belle. There was a shrewdness in Cheyenne's aqua eyes that belied the blond bombshell look she'd cultivated with a pair of sky-high wedge boots and a low-cut top that showed off a spectacular display of cleavage along with a gorgeous necklace of wire-wrapped crystals in sterling silver.

"Stephie says ya'll are helpin' her sort through those horrible nightmares she's been havin'," Cheyenne said, the concern lacing her tone sending Mag's BS-o-meter up another notch. Cheyenne might seem like the doting cousin, but Mag smelled the distinct, mingling scents of desperation and opportunism.

"Did you find anything?" Stephanie turned wide eyes on Mag and Clara.

Mag shook her head, "Nothing suspicious or out of place. No paperweight, no desk, no signs of a struggle. We're inclined to believe it was nothing more than a very vivid nightmare."

"That's what I keep tellin' her. I was home that night, and I'd have heard a commotion. Besides, it's not like there's a body, and no way could Stephie have gotten rid of all the evidence on her own." Cheyenne provided Mag the perfect opening to pepper her with questions.

Casting a sideways glance at her sister, Mag said, "You were there that night? Constance seemed to think you'd spent the evening with your boyfriend."

Cheyenne scoffed, "Constance thinks I'm out sowing wild oats if I'm not back in the house by eight and asleep by nine-thirty. I had a late class and then a group study session, and I got home 'bout ten-thirty. I knocked to check on Stephie, and Brad said she was sound asleep."

Cheyenne started to say something else, but snapped her mouth shut and cast a sideways glance at Stephanie, who didn't notice because she was lost in her own thoughts. Cheyenne was holding something back, and Mag intended to find out exactly what that might be.

"Stephanie, why don't you show Clara around? I know she's been dying to get a look at your herb garden. I'll sit back and get to know your cousin a little better. That is, if she doesn't mind chatting up an old lady for a few minutes." Mag said pointedly. Cheyenne nodded her assent, and as soon as Clara and Stephanie were out of earshot, turned to Mag with a look of appreciation.

"You'd fit right in down south, Ms. Balefire, with that ability to distract and divide." She stated wryly.

"I could sense you had something else to say, and that you didn't want your cousin to hear it," Mag said, cutting straight to the chase.

"You're right about that. I know old Connie thinks the sun rises 'n sets with Brad, but to be honest it didn't surprise me as much as it did her or Stephanie when he bailed. You see, on my way to my bedroom that night, I heard Brad pacin' the hallway, talkin' about meetin' up somewhere. I heard him say eleven o'clock was perfect, and I could hear the person on the other end say goodbye. It was a woman, I'm sure of it. It just seemed like adding insult to injury to tell poor Stephie about it. I mean, he'd already gone, and there didn't seem much point in makin' things worse. But now she's all up in a tizzy thinkin' she might have done something to hurt him, and well, I guess you could say we're in muddy water."

Mag couldn't have agreed more. The waters certainly were muddied, and so was her opinion of Cheyenne. She seemed to genuinely care about her cousin, and to have Stephanie's best interests at heart, but there was something about her that grated.

"Was that the first time you'd wondered about his intentions?" Mag inquired. It seemed as though she might have found one person who wouldn't mince words, and she intended to use the discovery to her advantage.

Cheyenne shook her head. "I thought he was perfect for Steph when she first brought him home, but lately he's seemed a bit … off, I guess. On edge. And he's been takin' more private calls than normal. He mighta been dealing with weddin' plans, though, for all I know."

Her explanation came to an abrupt halt when a scruffy young man appeared on the path from the direction of the house. "Bas! You're late." Cheyenne admonished, but her wide, besotted smile belied any real irritation.

"Sorry, babe." Bas apologized lazily, wrapping his arms around Cheyenne and grabbing her rear end with both hands in a way that made Mag supremely uncomfortable. She knew he'd seen her, because they'd made eye contact for a brief moment while Mag sized him up and came to nearly the same conclusion as Constance.

Bas sported a long mane of slightly greasy hair tied into a bun on the top of his head. That alone was enough for Mag to consider him a delinquent, but the smarmy look in his bright green eyes was what sealed the deal.

Oh yes, he was handsome in an alternative sort of way, with a strong jawline and perfectly symmetrical features. It was his attitude that made him unattractive, changed what would have been a nice smile into a condescending sneer and highlighted the cockiness in his postured stance.

Cheyenne waved her goodbye to Mag, tossing a distracted, "take care of my cousin," over her shoulder while following Bas back down the path.

"Kids these days, indeed." Mag muttered to herself, grateful she'd long since left the stupidity of her own youth behind.

Chapter Eight

Leaving Stephanie with Constance, Clara followed her sister outside. "You drive," she said, shocking Mag with the suggestion. Most of the time, it was Mag who experienced flashes of intuition and insight when it came to finding evidence and solving crimes, but it seemed Clara had the tingles about this case.

After talking to Cheyenne, Mag decided Brad had left Stephanie for some other woman, but Clara's gut said otherwise and she was willing to defend that position.

Mag would call it a flight of fancy or wishful thinking, and she might be right. Clara didn't think so, though. She couldn't understand why when it came to intuition, Mag trusted her own beyond reason, but was quick to discard anyone else's feelings without remorse.

Listening to her prattle on about cold feet and cheating louts, Clara tamped down her irritation the same way she always did, without worrying whether at some point, it might come bursting out in the exact kind of magical display she tried so hard to avoid.

"Stop here!" When Clara practically shouted in her ear, Mag jumped and yanked the bus to a halt.

"Are you trying to kill me? I think I just had a heart attack."

"Sorry." Feet hitting the pavement, Clara called back over her shoulder, "I need some things from the grocery store. You go on ahead and I'll walk home when I'm done." She didn't think Mag had noticed the tall— and yes, handsome—figure of Stephanie's uncle disappearing through the automatic sliding doors.

"Get me some ice cream," Mag ordered and Clara knew what was coming next. "Butter pecan if they have it. I'll wait."

Other than to satisfy that niggling of her intuition and a powerful need to talk to the man again, there hadn't been anything Clara needed. And yet she picked up a basket, slung the handle over her elbow, and made her way along, taking a surreptitious glance down each aisle as she passed.

She found him staring at the ice cream selection in the freezer section, and managed to make meeting him there look like a happy coincidence. Judging by the way his eyes lit up when he saw her, it wasn't much of a tough sell.

When he reached out to shake, she put her hand in his.

"A lot of choices," he gestured toward the shelves. "I remember when there was one brand to choose from and maybe five flavors on a good day. Now it's fat free, sugar free, double churned—whatever that means—and four kinds of chocolate. Frozen yogurt, gelato. How am I supposed to choose?"

Clara's laugh rolled out, rich and warm like the rest of her. "I'm going for the old standby, butter pecan. It's my si … mother's favorite." Flustered because he hadn't let go of her hand, she almost forgot the cover story she and her sister used to explain away the difference in their apparent ages.

"Don't you have a favorite?" John asked, the well-worn lines around his eyes crinkling in an unexpectedly attractive way.

"Anything with caramel. And you?"

His smile sent another shiver over Clara's skin. "Mint chocolate chip, but this isn't for me. Cheyenne called to tell me Stephanie had a hard day. The kind that requires boatloads of ice cream and other mysterious things women do to get over a breakup, so here I am. Tell me what to buy."

"Go with the good stuff. Start with the full fat, extra churned. Go for anything that says double chocolate on it. Then, this caramel gelato with chocolate shavings on the top, and the rainbow sherbet, and something with coffee in it. That should cover the bases. Oh and if you really want to earn some brownie points, buy brownies." In times like these, a little self-indulgence never hurt.

"Brownies it is. Though I don't see how any of this is going to heal a broken heart." The shadow that crossed his face said more than words, and Clara suspected he was thinking of his late wife. Time was the only cure for that type of loss.

"You'd be surprised at the healing effects of copious amounts of chocolate." Clara recovered from her private thoughts quickly, though it took her a fraction of a second to remember what she was supposed to be replying to. "I know Stephanie has had quite a shock, but she'll be all right, eventually."

John's face clouded over, "She'll survive and find someone more suited."

The statement didn't come as a surprise to Clara. After all, John thought of Stephanie as his own little girl, and all father figures are suspicious of the other men in their daughter's lives. But that didn't mean she'd let the statement pass without digging for more details.

"What was wrong with Brad? I don't mean to pry—well, actually I do." Clara knew her tone sounded flirtatious, but she found herself unable to tamp it down.

Frowning, John shifted his weight and rested his shopping basket on his other hip, "I'm not insinuating that good people can't come from bad circumstances, or that Brad didn't try to overcome a disadvantaged childhood."

This time when the tingle came, it had more to do with what John had to say than his sexy manner. Worse, this jangle along her nerves came with a sense of dread.

"I know Stephanie would not approve, but when things started getting serious between them so quickly, I hired a private detective, and learned some disturbing information about Brad's family."

"And what did you find?" Caught between the parts of her that wanted to get closer to him and the parts that wanted to recoil because he'd gone behind Stephanie's back, Clara felt a little crazed.

She missed part of what he had to say because her brain kept providing good reasons for what he'd done and then countering with all the ways it constituted betrayal. How could she be attracted to someone like him, and how could she not?

"—was convicted. Bigamy is a class E crime, and the judge gave him the maximum sentence. When he got out of jail six months later, Scott Graham had lost both wives, his kids, and his job. He was on the hook for child support times three. He'd borrowed the money to pay his fine from Brad's grandfather and when my investigator dug a little deeper, it turned out Scott took the money and ran. Never saw any of his kids again, including Brad."

"And you think Bradley takes after his father."

"I'd hoped not, for Stephanie's sake, but now I'm not so sure. I didn't have the heart to tell her anything about it, and it doesn't matter anymore, anyway." John shook his head., "Mason seems to think he was siphoning money from Pets Alive, and temporarily pulled their funding while they review the books. Neither conclusion makes me feel any better about the situation."

"I'm sorry things turned out the way they did." Almost instantly, the niggling doubts that had started to creep into Clara's head dissipated. Rich people had problems—and solutions—she'd never understand, but she understood that John had felt it was his duty to protect Stephanie. And how could she fault him for that?. Sizzling jolts of energy radiated from his hand to hers and didn't stop there. Even her toes felt the sparks as they curled inside her shoes.

"Nothing for you to be sorry about.," John shook his head., "Everything happens for a reason. At least, that's what I try to tell myself. Take this, for instance, you and I being in the same place at the same time, buying ice cream."

Clara wasn't about to tell him the reason for that was that she'd stalked and cornered him in the frozen-foods aisle, and instead felt the blush creeping up to her cheeks as, to her surprise, she let out a breathy response., "Yes, I'd call that a happy coincidence." Despite what he insinuated he'd done, she wanted him.

John smiled, and once again Clara found herself drowning in his sparkling eyes. When he spoke, his voice had gone all husky and shy., "I don't suppose you'd want to repeat it, on purpose this time. For instance, at dinner say, tomorrow night?"

Now that she was being put on the spot, Clara was torn. On the one hand, involving herself personally with a member of Stephanie's family when she and Mag were only supposed to be solving the mystery of her disappearing fiancé had to be a conflict of interest. On the other hand, it wasn't as though they'd been hired, or were receiving any kind of compensation. It was a favor for a friend, and that was that.

"I'd love to."

"Perfect, I'll pick you up at seven o'clock." John smiled that delicious smile again, and Clara felt like a damsel from a Jane Austen novel.

The number of decades since she'd felt this way about any man could be counted on one hand, but that was still a long time for an itch to develop and Clara had one. One she wanted to scratch with this man. She could admit that to herself.

She might have admitted it to him, too, if she'd had the chance.

"Hello Clara." Norm McCreery, Harmony's mayor, had been harboring a crush on the younger Balefire sister since the pair had moved to town. An unrequited crush. Oh, he was nice enough and not bad looking, but not the kind to set a woman's toes on fire with nothing more than a touch. He did have impeccable timing, though.

"Mr. McCree...ry." Drat that Mag. She'd called him Mayor McCreepy so many times the name had become stuck in Clara's head. Still, she hoped the formal greeting would be enough to convince John that there was nothing romantic going on there. But when he released her hand, she wasn't sure if it was only to offer it to Norm, or her plan had failed.

"If you'll excuse me, I have to go." Clara yanked open the freezer, grabbed the first carton of ice cream on the shelf, and left the two men staring after her. If she'd bothered to turn and look, she'd have seen identical expressions of admiring interest.

Rounding the corner of the aisle, she held the ice cream container to her heated cheek for a second, then took a good look at the label. Mag would be eating fat-free, plain old vanilla instead of butter pecan, and Clara would never hear the end of it.

Preferring privacy above all else, Mag lived in what looked from the outside like an overgrown shed tossed together from materials pulled out of a dumpster. Dusty cobwebs—or the illusion of them anyway—, coated the windows, and the whole thing appeared to lean precariously to the left.

From the inside, Mag enjoyed a clear view of the river from a pristine bay window, in her perfectly cluttered, bedecked- with- doilies, Victorian-styled parlor.

Too fussy for Clara's tastes, the decor suited Mag right down to the ground and was completely at odds with her reputation. It was there where, later that night, unable to sleep, Clara broke one of Mag's cardinal rules.

She knocked on the door sometime after midnight, and entered without waiting for her sister's reply. Mag knew something was on her mind, but waited patiently as Clara wandered about her living room and gravitated to a display of family heirlooms covering the mantle above the fireplace. Clara touched a gentle finger to her father's gold pocket watch, and wiped a tear from her cheek.

"I don't know if it's the time of year, or Roma being here, or maybe just her mention of the history of this house, but I can't stop thinking about Mum and Papa. I know you hate talking about them, but I'm telling you right now, Maggie, I can't keep indulging this gag order of yours. Please,." Clara pleaded, the desperation in her voice zinging like an arrow straight through Mag's heart.

Mag repositioned herself on the settee where she'd been knitting, and returned her needles to the bag at her feet., "It's not that I don't want to talk about them, Clarie. It just hurts. What I can't understand is how you could ever forgive her. You were always Mum's golden child—future Keeper, model witch—and I took solace in Papa's constant encouragement. He's the only one who understood my wanderlust, and part of me died right along with him. But she was supposed to stick around and help us through it. Instead she just bailed." Mag stared at her sister, the pain evident in her twisted expression.

"I was just as angry as you were, but for Goddess's sake Maggie, she died of a broken heart. It's not as though we were kids who couldn't fend for ourselves. All I ever wanted was a love like that—a true love—and I waited centuries for it before Richard walked into my life. When he left, I finally understood how Mum felt. Are you telling me you've honestly never cared about another human being that much?" What Clara really wanted to know was whether her sister had ever cared about a man that much, but she chose not to push her luck.

Mag raised an eyebrow., "I care about you that much, Clarie. And you've never given me a reason not to respect your choices. What you did with your loss was become stronger. You stuck around to raise your daughter. You let the hole in your heart heal over into a manageable scar, and realized that there are very few men capable of living up to the example Papa set for us. Do you think I'm proud of myself for running scared? Maybe if I'd stuck around, been there for you and Sylvana, your relationship wouldn't have devolved past the point of no return."

Mag's words shocked Clara; she'd had no idea her sister blamed herself for anything that had happened. "Don't blame yourself for my mistakes. Families are complicated things. When expectations get all tied up with the notion of unconditional love, we forget how easy it is to hurt each other when our defenses are down."

"Yes, Clarie, it certainly is." Mag agreed. "All the same, I've made mistakes myself. Hopefully, we have plenty of time to make up for them."

Clara hugged her sister and padded back to bed with a lighter heart, praying to the Goddess Mag was right.

Chapter Nine

Clothed in the rich reds and golds of autumn with the clock tower standing out in sparkling white, the town of Harmony could have posed for a jigsaw puzzle or a calendar shoot. The Big Spurwink river ran down behind the town with a curve as graceful as a lady's spine.

Mag spun the wheel and turned left when she should have turned right.

Eyebrow raised, Clara asked, "Did you forget the way home?"

"No. I'm getting some decent ice cream, and you're paying. You owe me." Clara had been right; her sister was still unimpressed with her ice cream-related lapse, though Mag admitted running into John had been fortuitous, especially after Clara had relayed the conversation regarding Brad's father. "Dairyland closes in a few days anyway, and I want another cone of that pumpkin maple swirl before they do." Mag flicked the VW's blinker to indicate a right-hand turn into the parking lot.

"It looks like we're not the only ones with dessert on the brain," Clara noted the line that trailed nearly back to the road. After less than a year living in the small town of Harmony, she recognized a number of the people milling about the parking lot. She waved to a couple of frequent customers, then turned into a space near the back and killed the spell that kept the sound of the minibus engine revving.

Even Mag, who was loathe to socialize, had become known and respected for her brusque personality and ability to locate rare antiques. Upon being spotted by one of the members of crochet club, where Mag routinely declared her disdain by clinking knitting needles together loudly, Clara was left alone to wait for her turn at the window. She pulled her sweater around her, shivering, and was a little sad to realize this truly was going to be her last ice cream cone of the season.

Somebody tapped on her shoulder, and when she turned to see who had summoned her, she was pleasantly surprised to find Evelyn St. James, the latest "Evelyn" in a long family line of bakers whose secret recipe yielded the airiest, most delicious yeast donuts in four counties.

Since becoming the reigning Evelyn and taking over where her mother and grandmother had left off, the youngest St. James had expanded Evelyn's Bakery into a coffee shop and eatery with her inventive recipes. In recent months, she'd begun frequenting Balms and Bygones, picking Clara's herbalist brain for unusual pairing combinations.

"Hey, how did they do?" Clara asked without preamble.

Evelyn grinned. "My grilled cheese donut went like gangbusters, but your cardamom and blueberry one was the biggest shocker."

"You've got another idea brewing, don't you? I can tell." Clara's mouth was already watering at the thought.

"I'm not sure, but it involves crushed up Fruity Pebbles and marshmallows. Something like a rainbow rice crispy treat, but in donut form. If that makes any sense."

"Sounds delicious to me. I'm available as a taste tester anytime." Clara wiggled her eyebrows.

Evelyn laughed. "It's a date, then. Hey, did I see you headed up toward Huffington Manor the other day?"

Clara sensed an opportunity to find out a little bit more about the public opinion of Stephanie and her family, and nodded. "You sure did. It turns out we have a friend in common, but I only recently met Stephanie. She seems nice." Clara let the simple statement hang in the air, and waited patiently for Evelyn's response.

"Yes, she certainly is. Always has been. You ought to take a look at her herb garden. Boggles the mind, and I've heard she's even got a shed back there that's built to look like a gypsy wagon. Not exactly in keeping with the rest of the grounds, but who's going to stop her? Can you imagine having all that money and no family to share it with? At least, no family to speak of." Evelyn rambled, her long hours behind the counter at the bakery having accustomed her to gossiping without remorse.

"Actually, I did get a chance to see the wagon, and I've got to admit it's pretty cool." Clara wondered if anyone knew just how appropriate the wagon was, considering Stephanie's maternal lineage, but kept the thought to herself.

Mag joined the line in time to hear what Evelyn had said and butted into the conversation. "It's sad, isn't it? I'll give credit where it's due: Stephanie seems lovely," she commented, catching on to Clara's intention without the necessity of a discussion.

"She certainly fits the description of 'poor little rich girl' to a T." Evelyn remarked.

"We met her uncle John while we were there," Mag added.

Clara's cheeks pinked, and she remained silent at Mag's mention of the man.

Evelyn gave a little hum. "John Masters hasn't been quite the same since he lost Buffy. She liked to spread the wealth just as much as the rest of the Huffingtons, but he's a bit tight with the purse strings."

Mrs. Green, the nosy neighbor who lived next door to Balms and Bygones piped up, shoving herself further in line to join the group. "He's turning into an old Scrooge. Used to be quite the troublemaker, that man. Course, that was ages ago."

"He might act like a Scrooge, but he looks like an old-timey movie star." Evelyn's eyes misted over. "Reminds me of Marlon Brando. Well-preserved, that's for sure." She wiggled her eyebrows and the color in Clara's cheeks went from pink to bright red.

She wished the fall breeze hadn't eliminated the excuse of hot weather, and hoped nobody noticed her reaction. Knowing her sister's keen eye had picked up every nuance of her expression, Clara knew she'd be teased mercilessly later.

"What kind of trouble did he make, exactly?" Mag asked before Clara had the chance to.

"Oh, nothing truly scandalous," Mrs. Green said, flapping a hand. "Helped steal the Harmony High School mascot before the Homecoming game his senior year."

"And there was something else, too." Evelyn snapped her fingers as if it would help bring back the memory. "Remember?"

"I only remember him spending a lot of time out at the pits." Mrs. Green couldn't dredge up the details, either.

Clara and Mag exchanged a confused look. "At the pits?" Clara asked.

"The gravel pits out on the western edge of town. Used to be what we called Lookout Point, because you can see the river from the top of the ravine. Kids like to take their dirt bikes out there in the summer, and in the winter it's all about the snowmobiles. I'd imagine most of what they're racing over is old beer cans and empty wine cooler bottles. Chief Cobb's tried to put a stop to the partying, but since nobody's ever been seriously injured he might as well be talking to a brick wall."

At the chance for new gossip, Mrs. Green lit up and leaned in close to absorb every detail. "Speaking of scandal, such a shame about Stephanie Huffington's young man."

"Yes," Evelyn continued, "Didn't you know? He left her in the middle of the night. Packed up and moved away, from what I heard."

"Any idea why?"

"It's a mystery, but it goes to show that money isn't everything."

When Clara opened her mouth to defend Stephanie, Mag dragged her away with some lame excuse.

"What are you doing?" Clara snapped, trying to pull her arm free. "They're talking about her like she did something wrong."

"I know, Clarie. But you're not going to convince anyone by arguing when we don't know the truth. There are any number of reasons he might have left."

Taking the driver's seat when they got back to the van, Clara paused a moment before turning the charmed key that ran the bus in lieu of a working motor. "Then let's find out why. We can protect Stephanie's good name and give her closure."

"And how do you propose we do that?" Mag barked.

"We'll go to the shelter where he worked. Ask some questions. It's what we do. Don't you think we should? We could go right now—it's probably still open." Clara eased out of the parking space and prepared to turn in that direction.

"It's going to have to wait until tomorrow. Did you forget we're expected at the full moon celebration tonight?"

Banging a hand on the steering wheel, Clara said, "I did forget, and worse, I was supposed to cook something for the potluck picnic after the ritual."

"There's a picnic? Or is it more like a cookout?" If it was a cookout, there might be hot dogs and Clara rarely let Mag have those at home. Something about having taken Sylvana to the plant on a school field trip and seeing what went into the making of them.

"All I know is Penelope called and asked me to bring broccoli slaw. Now that Hagatha's settled down—and I don't trust that as far as I could toss an elephant—Penelope seems quite pleased with herself. She practically ordered me to bring food."

Near to drooling, Mag focused on the food portion of the conversation. "If that's the one with the bacon and cheese in it, I'm with Penelope. You could make extra and put some in my fridge."

Dressed in their ritual garb and ready for what, for a witch, equates to a night on the town, there was no need for Mag and Clara to bother driving the five miles to Dawkin's woods, where the full-moon celebration was taking place that evening. Skimming was much faster, and would negate the necessity of driving while intoxicated by the swell of communal power that always accompanied these types of events.

For once, Mag was in a better mood than Clara, who had worn a sour-faced expression while donning her robes. Since she preferred a solitary practice, joining in coven politics usually raised Mag's hackles, but when it came time to commune with the Goddess, she could get on board with the extra kick of power. And there'd be food. Possibly hot dogs.

"What'd you do, swallow a bug?" Mag asked when even the sight of Jinx batting unsuccessfully at Whizzer's curious but incorporeal nose didn't nudge a smile from her sister's lips.

Clara heaved a big sigh. "Truthfully, I'm feeling a little sorry for myself. When Penelope asked us here, it was with the understanding that we'd be leading the coven. I spent twenty-five years encased in stone listening to the Port Harbor witches complain about Calypso Snodgrass, and now that I can work my magic again, I'm still finding myself stuck on the sidelines while Penelope Starr tries to shove Hagatha unceremoniously into retirement. It's frustrating, to say the least."

Mag let out a low whistle, "Clarie, I think that's about as honest as you've been on this particular topic. Buck up, little sister, and remember who you're dealing with. Old Haggie might be willing to step aside and let Penelope run the Moonstones into the ground, but she's kept a tight hold on the reins to the coven itself. This ought to be interesting, to say the least. The rest will work itself out eventually. Always does."

"And that's about as optimistic as I think I've ever seen you. Period. Okay, fine, I'll stop moping." Clara pasted a smile on her face, but it didn't quite reach her eyes. Mag wished there was something else she could say to lift her sister's maudlin spirits, but couldn't think of what, so she let it rest.

A few moments later, the pair landed with a soft thump at the edge of the woods, their feet touching down on a soft bed of moss. Through the trees, the faint glow of bobbing torches led Mag and Clara to a ring of stones filled with the charred remains of last month's gathering.

Clara, relishing the one responsibility she knew was still decidedly hers, fulfilled her duties as former Keeper of the Balefire and made a show of lighting the ritual fire. She conjured a bit of the flame from the tip of her finger, willing it to grow into a ball between her palms. A shower of sparks accompanied its trajectory into the pit, where it roared to life amongst the wide-eyed gasps of Harmony's underage magical community.

Mag settled into a seat with a proud smile playing across her lips. She could have done the same thing Clara had just accomplished, but it meant more to her sister. Once everyone settled in, Hagatha emerged from the shadows with as much pomp and circumstance as she could muster.

"The full moon, as you all should know, represents abundance and prosperity. It's a time when we celebrate Mother Earth, and by extension, all of the blessings she has bestowed upon us. The Goddess often works in mysterious ways, and sometimes she makes us fight for what we want. You all know the story of how witches were given the gift of near-immortality, right?"

A chorus of yeses fell from their collective lips, but their eyes remained locked on Hagatha, urging her to tell it again anyway. Hagatha spared no energy on her performance, honed from years of repetition and enhanced by the genuine joy it gave her to pass the legends of witchkind down through the generations. As far as she was concerned, books were for worms, while the oral nature of folklore helped paint a more vivid mental picture that drew in the listener and increased the retention of detail exponentially.

Hagatha's eyes sparkled as she circled the campfire and spoke to the small crowd of pint-sized witches and wizards sitting cross-legged on the ground in a circle around her feet. Their little faces held a mixture of avid curiosity and excitement as the elder witch stretched her arms wide and spun in circles while retelling the tale of the faerie prince who fell in love with a powerful witch.

"Thousands of years ago, the civil war between the Faerie courts of White and Black—Seelie and Unseelie—raged in the Faelands, on the verge of rolling over into the Earthly realm. The dark Unseelie deemed it 'unnatural' for the Fae to consort with other beings—especially witches and humans. That doesn't sound very fair, does it?" Hagatha paused to ask, noting the nods of all the little heads in answer to her question. Truthfully, she preferred children to adults, as they hadn't yet developed the level of cynicism that comes with age.

Mag and Clara, positioned themselves on one of the carved logs ringing the fire, listened with rapt attention. This story meant just a little more to them than it did to anyone else present, and it was the first time they'd experienced Hagatha's telling of it. In these moments, it was clear to see why she had been named High Priestess in the first place.

"One brave witch, Esmerelda, took matters into her own hands, crafting a special flame to protect against the Black Court. You see, her husband and his half-Fae sister had been killed in the battles, and Esmerelda was left alone with a young daughter, Bianca, to protect.

"When Unseelie prince Oberon came looking for the girl and laid eyes on the beautiful Esmerelda, he fell instantly in love and vowed to change his ways. At first, the feeling wasn't mutual—after all, the Unseelie were responsible for the heartache Esmerelda had experienced. Oberon didn't give up, and eventually Esmerelda returned his love and pleaded with her brother and sister witches to help banish the Unseelie from this realm once and for all."

With the crackling of the Balefire behind her, Hagatha's words seemed both ethereal and historical at the same time, weighted with the power of her years and position.

"Much of witchkind joined the fight, and with the help of Oberon and the Seelie race, eventually overcame the Dark Court and restored peace to the Faelands. In order to keep the Unseelie from returning to the Earthly realm, Esmerelda created a failsafe—a sacred flame that protected against the darkness."

Hagatha's eyes flicked first to Mag and then settled on Clara for an extra moment. "Do any of you know what flame I'm talking about?"

The children grinned and responded in unison, "It's the Balefire!"

"It certainly is—and we're lucky enough to have not one but two Balefire witches in our coven. It's a great honor." Tiny eyes widened, and Hagatha's theory on oral history was proven fact: none of the children present would forget the day they got to hear the legend of the Balefire in proximity to direct descendants of the famed Esmerelda.

"What about the rest?" Little Sadie Spellman piped up when Hagatha made a move to sit back in her seat.

Hagatha looked around at each child with exaggeratedly wide eyes. "You want to hear what happened next?"

"Yes!" Came the enthusiastic reply. They were like tiny sponges, soaking up whatever knowledge could be gleaned from listening to adults. Of course, you never knew when they'd spew the information back out, and it often occurred at the most inconvenient times. It was no wonder Hagatha felt a kinship to children, considering she suffered from the same affliction.

"Okay then. Prince Oberon—now King of the Fae—knew he couldn't live without the love of his life, and he also knew that the few years she had left weren't nearly enough. He used a considerable amount of Faerie magic to make Esmerelda immortal—and even offered her daughter, who by then had grown into a woman, the same gift. Only Bianca refused, instead striking a bargain that would benefit all of witchkind. I think we should let one of the Balefire sisters tell the rest, don't you?"

Mag poked Clara in the ribs. "You were Keeper—go for it."

"Well," Clara began, stepping forward, "Bianca made a vow to watch over the sacred flame, and pass the honor down through the generations, knowing that as long as the Balefire burned bright, the Unseelie would remain trapped in the Faelands. She implored King Oberon to amend his terms, and asked him to bestow prolonged life upon all witches in case the Balefire family line ever died out. He agreed, even though it meant that even he could never reenter the earthly realm. Esmerelda followed him back to the Faelands, and as far as anyone knows, they're still there, ruling to this very day." Clara gave a little nod and sat back down, allowing Hagatha to retake the stage.

"And that's why we all have a bit of Balefire burning in our hearth. Witch feeds flame, and flame feeds witch. It's why we have distributors who travel to the Keeper every year at Beltane, renew their connection to the Balefire, and spread its magic across the Earth. And of course, it's why we keep a low profile, and try not to reveal our magic to mortals."

Mag snorted quietly, finding the idea of Hagatha preaching about low profiles hilarious considering how many times she'd nearly outed the lot of them. When she and Clara had stepped into the Harmony coven, they was under the impression that Hagatha's give-a-damn had gone out the window, but after having dealt extensively with the High Priestess over the previous few months, it was clear they'd been hoodwinked, and not by Haggie.

Hagatha's actions didn't stem from a desire to expose the magical community—she'd simply come to the realization that most people don't believe even when the truth is staring them square in the face.

Coupled with a penchant for getting her geriatric self into troublesome situations, Hagatha tended to act without thinking. Still, Mag knew there was more to the story, but so far any attempt to discern Penelope's reasoning for summoning the sisters only to treat them with utter contempt had come up short.

After the dramatic conclusion of Hagatha's tale, and the feast which did, to Mag's delight, include hot dogs, the senior coven members left the children making s'mores under the supervision of the older kids, and receded to an adjacent clearing for some conversation of an official nature. It brought a smug smile to Mag's lips when she noticed the children skirted an arc around Penelope, some even turning their noses up at her when she spoke to even the teens as though they were toddlers.

"So, I heard you've made friends with Stephanie Huffington." Penelope made the statement with no preamble, and the way she spit it out made it seem like a question to which she was entitled an answer. Even in ritual attire, Penelope somehow managed to show off her glamoured cleavage, though why she bothered in a gathering of witches who could see the shriveled scoops of flesh underneath the façade, neither Mag nor Clara could understand.

Gertrude Granger, one of the few witches who had taken the time to get to know the Balefires, sidled up beside them and responded before Mag could open her mouth to spew vim and vinegar all over Penelope. "Don't see how that's any of your concern."

Penelope largely ignored Gertrude, whose red velvet robes trimmed in white fur—an homage to the

Christmas holiday Gertrude loved most and all year round—were an assault to the eyes and in particular Penelope's fashion sense, and spoke to Clara directly. Mag found it amusing that Penelope considered her sister the least volatile of the pair, and vehemently hoped that at some point in the future, Clara would show her how wrong she was on that count.

There was plenty of spice under Clara's sugary coating.

"Under normal circumstances, I couldn't care less who you socialize with, but we've been trying to get Stephanie Huffington to donate some funds to the Moonstones, and so far she's been less than cooperative." Penelope scowled.

"Maybe she just doesn't like you; did you ever think of that?" Mag couldn't hold back the snark.

Penelope shot her a dirty look and continued addressing Clara. "Josephine Huffington was a great supporter of the Moonstones, and Buffy carried on the tradition. Once she passed, the donations ceased. It would be a great boon if you could find out why, and see if we can get back in the Huffington's good graces. The future of the community center depends on it, and you know how important it is for the kids in this town to have something to do besides huff paint thinner and raid old Mr. Tate's strawberry fields."

As far as cover stories went, Clara couldn't find fault with the Moonstones. When Hagatha conceived the idea for the group, anonymity was more than necessary. The practice of burning witches at the stake was still popular, and groups of women with no purpose were suspect. Nowadays, there was less concern, but the civic side of the organization did so much good, the Harmony coven simply kept on keeping on.

"Don't you think this would be better coming from you, Penelope?" Clara asked, casting a sideways glance at the other witch. "It is, after all, part of the job you lobbied so hard to get, and you've made it quite clear how little use the Balefire sisters are to the community. Outside certain, shall we say, *unsavory* chores, that is. How could you trust us not to let out any secrets about the Moonstones you'd rather keep under wraps?"

"Pfft." Penelope dismissed Clara's pointed barb. "Jo Huffington knew all about the Moonstones, and I do mean *all about us.*"

Ah, Mag thought, that must be why Stephanie seemed so calm when they'd told her their secret.

"We'll have to think about it." She refused to commit to anything and made sure Clara did the same.

Chapter Ten

"Aren't you glad this place was on the way to the shelter?" A bag of chocolate donuts in one hand and molasses ones in the other, Clara juggled the two packages and waited for Mag to choose.

Located halfway between Port Harbor and Harmony, C&R's carried as eclectic a mix as Balms and Bygones, except it lay at the other end of the spectrum when it came to goods. Part grocery store, part restaurant, and part gas station, you could also purchase a full set of fishing gear including a license, browse through a selection of rental DVDs, or play a game of pool.

Considering the merits of both flavors, Mag made a quick decision. "Get both. And if they have any orange creme whoopie pies, I want one of those, too."

"Okie dokie," Clara said. A display of handmade Celtic-style jewelry had captured her attention. She'd already wrapped several sterling silver rings around her slim fingers and was holding them up to admire the effect. "I wonder if this artisan is local. These would sell really well at Balms and Bygones."

Mag agreed. "Ask for a card on our way out." She chose a pair of earrings and examined the beaten silver dangles. Good weight, nicely crafted. Excellent shelf appeal and would make a good addition to our product line."

Born of the necessity to cater to Mag's tiny bladder, the store made a perfect stopping point on the weekly trips back to the city to visit Clara's granddaughter Lexi. But it was the rustic charm and homemade potato salad that kept them coming back.

The witch's way of transport, magically skimming from one place to another, would have been easier, but driving offered the advantage of being able to stop and shop along the way. So, while Mag ruthlessly scoured shops and yard sales for rare antiques, Clara made it a point to hit every boutique from Harmony to Port Harbor.

"What do you think? Is it me?" Popping out from aisle behind the coolers, Mag sported a ball cap in pale blue with the words *Wicked Pissah* in white script across the front. To make matters worse, she'd added a sweatshirt featuring a moose wearing a googly-eyed lobster apron.

"Cute," Clara deadpanned, then whipped out her phone to snag a photo. "I'll blackmail you with this later."

"Can't see how. I'd have to give a rat's patootie for that to work, and I'm fresh out," Mag scoffed.

"You take the fun out of everything."

In addition to trying on various combinations of tourist wear, every time they visited the establishment,

Mag enjoyed the photo mounted on the wall behind the register. A panoramic view of the store's facade taken at least thirty years prior.

To her, the photo represented a real life version of the 'find the differences between these two photos' game. So far, other than updated trim colors, only one element appeared out of place: a set of hand hewn, three-foot-tall, wooden letters spelling out the store's name.

At some point in its history, CARS had become C&R's simply by replacing the A with an ampersand and adding an apostrophe.

Whether it had been a change of ownership, or merely the realization that Cars was a confusing name for a general store, Mag had no clue. But she did appreciate the thrifty nature of whoever had made the decision, and she found it comforting to be reminded that the more things change, the more they stay the same.

Under the wrinkles and flyaway hair, she was still a fun-loving girl with a penchant for getting herself into and out of impossible situations. That her insides didn't match her outsides was an unfortunate reality.

Unable to decide between three of the silver rings, Clara decided to buy them all and asked for more information about the jewelry maker.

The lanky boy manning the register, a youth named Shawn according to the tag pinned to his shirt, moved with all the speed of a slug. It took him nearly five minutes of rustling around behind the counter to figure out he couldn't find the artisan's card. Meanwhile, Mag hit the slushy machine.

"Red or blue, name your poison."

"I don't know why I love these so much," Clara commented, "You get all the flavoring out in a few sips and then all that's left is a cup full of tainted ice."

Mag grinned, "It's the same addictive ingredient the Colonel puts in his chicken, I swear."

Shawn emerged from the back room with a piece of paper. "I called my mom, and she said the woman's name is Cheyenne Bishop. I've got her number."

"No need, young man, we know Cheyenne." Shawn seemed a little irked that his efforts were going unappreciated as Mag waved away the slip of paper.

"Thank you, though," Clara said with a smile, but it did nothing to help the boy's mood.

Juggling the bag of goodies in her arms, Clara slid into the passenger's seat of the Volkswagen. "Weird coincidence, don't you think?"

"Not especially." Mag didn't believe in the concept of coincidence, but then again, she didn't believe in moon landings, either. "But I can see why Stephanie wants to send some funds Cheyenne's way. She's talented. Feckless idiot, Constance called her, but I don't think that's the case. She's just young and has gotten herself tangled up with a man far below her station."

"You've barely even met this guy and you're already condemning him, and based on one woman's opinion. A woman whose judgment you just questioned, no less. He could be perfectly nice." Clara's response should have chagrined her sister, but Mag had made enough concessions as of late.

"Trust me, barely was plenty. And you didn't meet him at all, so your opinion is invalid. When you do have the unfortunate experience of being introduced to that boob, you'll be eating a healthy serving of crow." Mag promised.

Clara let it drop and pointed to her right. "There's the sign for the shelter. Slow down and turn here."

"I see it, Miss Side Seat Driver." Mag put Cheyenne out of her mind to focus solely on the task ahead. Single-minded determination—that was the best way to get things done. Sometimes, Clara thought, it prevented her from seeing the bigger picture, but she'd discovered that when it came to her sister, there was never a good time to open a can of worms.

According to the search results on Clara's phone, the Pets Alive Animal Rescue sat on approximately ten acres and sheltered anywhere from five to twenty animals at a time. The grounds included a large red barn, a fenced-in area where six or seven dogs romped happily, and a corral of kennels shaded from the sun by a sturdily-built roofed awning. Everything received meticulous care, from the gravel parking area to the now-browning grassy play area. Only a few stray leaves from a nearly bare oak tree littered the lawn.

Mag, as was her custom, took in every detail in case there was a need to mentally reconstruct the setting later. Clara, meanwhile, absorbed the emotions radiating from the animals and humans present. Using her perceptions as a filter, she noted how her mind, body, and spirit felt about the surroundings. Together, the pair made a thorough and observant team.

Inside the office, a semi-circle chest-height counter provided a barrier to the area behind the scenes. Dogs barked in rotation. As soon as one stopped, another started up. Mag's nose wrinkled at the thought of having to listen to that racket all day long.

When the harried-looking woman popped up from behind the counter, Clara recognized her as one of the trio of young coven members Mag had dubbed Double Bubble, Toil, and Trouble.

"Can I help you?" Winifred Owens asked. The name came back to Clara with a snap. "Oh, it's you two. Are you looking for a dog?"

"No." Clara replied wistfully. "I love dogs, but Pyewacket would have a fit."

"Tell me about it. My Nixie gives me the silent treatment after every shift, but I love my job. Where else am I going to get paid to snuggle puppies?"

Hitting her chit-chat limit, Mag interrupted.

"We're looking for Bradley Graham." She declined to say why, but maintained the facade of having no idea Brad no longer worked at Pets Alive.

That caught Winnifred's interest. "Bradley?" The way she growled his name out from between clenched teeth gave a pretty good indication of her feelings for the man.

"Unfortunately, Bradley no longer works here. He resigned and left us in the lurch. We've all been working overtime, and it's going to take weeks to find a suitable replacement."

"Did he happen to provide a forwarding address?" Clara asked innocently.

"No, there wasn't one included in his resignation letter." Winifred shook her head. "Don't repeat this." Leaning forward, she pitched her tone low.

Clara thought to herself how nice it was to live in a town where people didn't hesitate to tell each other's business to virtual strangers. Of course, it was one thing when you were attempting to unearth information, and quite another when you were the subject of the loose lips.

Eyes sliding sideways as if to check for eavesdroppers, she announced, "But there's *talk*. It came as a shock. Running the shelter seemed like a passion project for him and none of us thought he would just up and leave."

With that non-explanation, the young witch cemented Mag's opinion that Toil was a better name for her since it took a lot of work to get her to come to a point.

"What kind of talk?"

"Brad was working on a long-range plan for expansion, thanks to Stephanie Huffington's generous donation. If he'd stayed, we were on track to double the number of animals we could help by the end of next year. It's important work. Now, there's talk we might be shutting down instead. We're all wondering if he got caught doing something shifty, because the funds should still be available. I can't imagine what else could have drawn him away, especially now."

Finally, something Mag could get her teeth in to. "Do you have any evidence? Have you seen or heard anything suspicious?"

Winifred, realizing she might have said too much, snapped her mouth shut and only shook her head.

"Look you—" Coming in hot, Mag would have steamrollered right over the younger witch if Clara hadn't jabbed her with an elbow and stepped in to smooth things over.

Fixing a reassuring smile on her face, she troweled it on thick. "I can tell you have …" Her voice dropped to a whisper and Clara glanced around as if to make sure no one was listening even though there was no one else in the building. "Strong magic. It makes you a good judge of character, and that's why your opinion would be so useful to figuring out why Bradley left so suddenly. We're worried about him, so is his fiancée, and I can tell you are, too."

Which was nothing less than the truth on all counts.

Delighted surprise bloomed over Winifred's face and Clara caught herself wondering about the younger witch's history. Had no one remarked on her potential before? Maybe it was time to get to know the individual members of her current coven a little better.

More kindly, now, Clara asked, "Do you think Brad was stealing from the shelter?"

Winifred paused. "I don't know. If you'd asked me that before he left, I'd have said no and not even thought twice. Now, I can't help wondering what was going on behind the scenes."

A quiet suggestion from Mag. "Trouble in paradise?"

"You mean with Stephanie?" Winifred seemed surprised and Mag nodded. She shook her head so hard her earrings swung. "Impossible. I've never seen a man so besotted with a woman. It was enough to make me think there might be a few good ones left in the pack."

Resting an elbow on the counter, Clara wondered what the chances were of Winifred letting them take a look around the office. "It's probably nothing."

"Why, what have you heard? I know there was a phone call for him on the office line a week or so before he left. A woman who didn't want to leave her name, but that's not unusual. We get sales calls all the time and I figured it was just someone else trying to hit the top guy in the chain of command."

"Well, we—"

The sound of another vehicle pulling up outside had Winifred checking the clock. "I'm sorry, I have an appointment to take this family through the shelter. They lost their dog in the spring, and now they're feeling like it's time to find a new fur baby. This is the best part of my job, watching people fall in love with a new companion."

A little misty-eyed, Winifred rounded the counter to welcome the new arrivals. "Come back anytime. I'll let you know if anything important about Brad comes to mind."

On the way back out the door, Mag nearly took a nasty fall when her cane got tangled in a rake leaning against the side of the building. "Ouch! That wasn't there before."

"I'm so sorry, ma'am." A lanky red-headed man in faded overalls quickly gathered his tools. "I'll get these out of your way." He walked with a limp, his left foot dragging slightly behind him, but it didn't seem to slow him down much.

"I'm okay, really. It's no big deal." Mag replied, loathe to be treated as the fragile old lady she appeared to be.

The man seemed grateful Mag was all right, and began chatting nervously. "Name's Tommy. I'm the gardener, and I was just finishing up the last of the fall tasks. Winter will be here before you know it. Farmer's Almanac says it's going to be a doozie. Did you ladies find what you were looking for?"

Mag winked at Clara and replied, "No, not exactly."

"There's been a rise in the number of surrenders lately, at least that's what I've heard. I'm not exactly in the loop, of course, I'm just the gardener. But I got my Maisie here, and she's just the best service dog I could have asked for." His face lit up and he snapped his fingers to call the golden lab to his side.

"Are you a war veteran, Tommy?" Mag asked, her curiosity getting the best of her while she returned the dog's intelligent, but gentle gaze. Never before had she felt so thoroughly assessed by an animal, and it unsettled her slightly.

"Yes, ma'am. Two tours in Iraq, till I got my leg blown off. I was lucky." Lucky was a stretch, as far as Mag was concerned, but she understood the sentiment.

"How long have you been working here?" she asked.

"Going on two years now. It's not easy to find a good job these days, but they let me work around my appointments and I get to bring my best girl to work with me. Couldn't ask for anything more."

"Did you happen to know Bradley Graham before he resigned?" Mag pried.

Tommy nodded. "Sure did. He's the one who hired me. Things have been hard around here, him leaving so suddenly."

He caught the expression on Mag's face and qualified. "Not for me, just in general. More work for everyone. Can't say I blame him though, who would want to work if they didn't have to? I'd sit home with Maisie all day if I could."

"Is that what he's doing? Did you see him before he quit?"

"No, and that was a little odd, if you ask me. Whole thing seems off. He didn't strike me as the kind of guy who would sneak out the back door. I just figured he cashed in his meal ticket. That girlfriend of his is loaded. But then again, what do I know? After all, I'm just the gardener." Tommy repeated for the third time. "You ladies have a nice day."

With that, he settled a rake in the wheelbarrow, grabbed the handles, and moved off to continue his work for the day, whistling for Maisie to follow.

"I'm driving." Clara announced in a tone that brooked no refusal, and ignored Mag's mutters of protest.

"Interesting how she corroborated Cheyenne's story, no?" Contemplating the coating of sugar on her fingertips, Mag tried to decide whether to lick them clean or eat another chocolate donut.

Clara spared her attention from driving to glance over at her sister. "Is that what you got from what Winnie said?"

"Well, yeah, didn't you think it was convenient that he's getting calls from women at work and on his personal line?"

For whatever reason, Clara felt compelled to defend Brad. "Oh, so now it's women. Honestly, Mag, you've condemned him without a shred of evidence, and you're turning more cynical by the day. The caller could have been a family member, or any number of other innocent women, for that matter."

Several chocolate crumbs flew out of Mag's mouth with the force of her response. "Or he had a side piece and was out for what he could get from Stephanie. We've never even met the man, so how am I supposed to form an opinion of him? And I'm not a cynic. We've been told there's danger lurking, and there's a man missing. I'm only looking at the facts."

"Or making them up to suit yourself."

"At least I'm not ignoring half of what people tell me. You hear the good things and discard the rest." Never would she admit it, but Mag admired Clara's ability to believe the best of everyone.

"You're making me out to be a Pollyanna type and that couldn't be further from the truth," Clara growled. "I'm not blind to people's faults; I simply choose to believe that most can rise above them." And with that, silence reigned until the VW rocked to a halt in front of Balms and Bygones.

Turning in her seat, Clara shot Mag a stern look. "Why can't you just be nice? That poor woman has had more heartache and loss in her life than anyone her age should have had to face. If she's been dumped, she didn't deserve it, and rubbing it in isn't going to win you any points. If something worse has happened to Brad, you're going to feel like a complete jerk later. I'm trying to save you from your baser impulses."

Sullen, Mag muttered, "I'm only telling it like it is."

"Well, don't."

The car door slammed behind Clara and neither sister was too happy with the other when they went inside.

The butterflies in Clara's stomach felt like they'd evolved into pterodactyls, and by the time she'd emerged from the shower to begin picking an outfit for her date with John, she'd nearly talked herself into calling to cancel.

She took a look around, checking for the presence of any male ghosts that might make the prospect of getting dressed feel like taking part in a peep show, but the only presence in her bedroom was Mag. Sprawled out on the bed with Jinx curled up against her side purring contentedly, it reminded Clara of when they were teenagers, getting ready for what then constituted a wild night out. Thankfully, this evening would not include a barn raising or skinny-dipping at the lake. At least, she doubted it anyway.

"I hope you're not planning on wearing that towel turban on your date," Mag teased with a grin. Her comment was returned with a look that was meant to be stern, but ended up looking pathetic due to the bundle of nerves that was Clara.

"I'm just joking with you, relax." Mag rolled her eyes.

"How am I supposed to relax? I haven't been on a date in decades."

"What? You worried you've started to grow cobwebs over your—"

"Don't even finish that sentence, Margaret Balefire." Clara admonished, but she couldn't hold back a snort of laughter.

"Why are you so nervous, anyway? You've got two hundred years on this guy. It isn't as though you're inexperienced, or some silly young girl who doesn't know her butt from a hole in the ground. You're an intelligent, beautiful woman, and I promise you he's having a bigger anxiety attack than you are."

Clara wondered if Mag had accidentally taken an anti-snark pill, so unused was she to her sister being this nice.

"I doubt it—at least he's dated during this century," Clara replied, her words running together as she tried to apply mascara and talk at the same time.

"Just be happy someone *wants* to take you on a date. Trust me, you'll miss it when you reach your crone phase and nobody gives you a second glance. We're only four years apart, Clarie, for crying out sideways. I should still be a healthy, virile woman, not an old bag of bones." Mag lamented. It wasn't much more than she'd ever said on the subject, but it was the first time Clara hadn't had to pry Mag's feelings out of her with a metaphorical crowbar.

"I had no idea you had any desire for a relationship," Clara said, feeling a little bad for her sister. "Don't give up. I'm sure there's a man out there for you somewhere." She hoped like heck she didn't say the wrong thing. You could never tell with Mag.

"It's not about wanting a relationship," Mag said, flopping onto the bed as much as her stiff joints and aching back would allow. "I never wanted that, not really. I wanted adventures and lovers and excitement. Now I've got antiques and bunions and a bum hip. Sometimes I think it would have been better if that Raythe had just taken me out. I never intended to get old—I figured I'd go down swinging in a fiery blaze. What that thing did to me was almost worse than killing me. Now all I have to look forward to is more centuries feeling like this." She indicated her prematurely wrinkled face and pear-shaped figure.

Mag had never possessed the same classic beauty as her sister. She'd always been a little taller, her features a little more angular and severe—what you might call handsome—but she'd had the same wide hazel Balefire eyes and symmetrical nose, and a ferocity for life that cast a unique beauty on her face. Margaret Balefire had been a force to be reckoned with, with just as many suitors as Clara had. Only difference was, it was usually the bad-boy type that went for Mag, and that was how she'd liked it. No commitments, no strings.

"Oh, Maggie, that's the saddest thing I've ever heard." Clara made a note to herself to talk to Hagatha about the effect honey pixie hormones had had on her sister. If they put their heads together, they might find a magical cure for her premature aging.

Mag scowled. "I'm not looking for pity, so stop that right now. I'm just telling it like it is. You wanted to know what's going on inside my head, you want to know how I *feel* about things all the time. I'm happy we're getting the chance to reconnect, but sometimes it feels like I'm watching you live life from the sidelines."

In fact, it felt like she was doing it right that very moment, watching Clara get ready to meet a man she was excited about. It made her happy, but that little green monster kept poking his head out of the shadows, threatening to burst onto the scene at any second.

Clara sighed, and kept her tone light. "Now you know how it felt to be me all those years, sitting around doing nothing but keeping the home fires burning."

"That's a cop-out and you know it, Clarie. Keepers can still live a full life, and you know just as well as I do you weren't chained to the hearth by anything more than your own sense of obligation. I'm truly glad to see you taking a chance. One of us sure as heck should. And stop right there, that dress is perfect."

"You think so?" Clara twirled in front of the mirror, applied a final coat of lipstick, and pronounced herself ready. If only those pterodactyls would stop twirling around inside her stomach, everything would be perfect.

John's eyes widened in appreciation when Clara descended the front steps outside Balms and Bygones. She'd let her chestnut hair fall in waves around her face, highlighting the amber flecks in her wide-set green eyes. Having come of age in a time before women were expected to flaunt themselves without any sense of propriety, she'd decided on a simple outfit of leggings and a long, loose-fitting button-down blouse under a cardigan. A belt to match the flat-heeled boots she wore cinched the top at her waist, and the silver jewelry from Cheyenne's collection elevated the look to date-worthy.

"Wow, you look … beautiful." John stuttered as he took her hand and led her down the walkway. She didn't have a chance to tell him how handsome he looked in the crisp cornflower-blue oxford shirt that showed off his well-built shoulders and made his brown eyes look like molten chocolate, because she was distracted by the sleek classic sports car parked at the curb.

"Is that an E-Type Jag? Looks like a '64."

It gave Clara much pleasure to note the surprised expression on his face. Men were always shocked when women knew anything about cars, though she could never fathom why they couldn't understand how a shiny, finely-tuned machine might appeal to members of both genders.

The fact that she could remember when the sporty E-Type hit the showroom floor for the first time, back in 1961, was something she'd keep to herself.

There were only a few restaurants in the small town of Harmony, and when John turned right out of Clara's driveway, she started to get a little concerned, "We aren't going to the Oarhouse are we?" She asked with an edge in her voice.

"Nope, I thought we could try something a little more my speed. It's a surprise. Or, at least I think it will be. What's wrong with the Oarhouse? They've really upped their game since they changed the name."

Clara laughed, relieved, "Yeah, the Harpy's Hideaway was colorful, but probably not great for the tourist business. Though, depending on what kind of tourists you're trying to attract, that might not be the case. Don't get me wrong, their food is fantastic, and the lobster rolls are to die for, but I don't think I can ever set foot in that place again after what happened during the canoe race."

Realization dawned on John, and he was instantly contrite. "Of course, the murder. You do seem to find yourself in some interesting situations for a small-town shop owner, I must say."

Hoping 'small-town shop owner' wasn't a euphemism for something even less flattering, Clara decided to brush past what felt like an insult and give John the benefit of the doubt. "Yes, I suppose that's true."

Over the next ten minutes, Clara learned that John enjoyed an eclectic mix of hobbies including para-sailing and Tai Chi, and though technically retired, he still went in to work five days a week because he truly cared about the charitable causes Huffington Foundation backed.

She explained, as much as she could explain while leaving coven politics at the door, how she and Mag had wound up moving to Harmony and opening Balms and Bygones. Those ten minutes were enough to make her realize that having to hide the details of her entire life might make the evening more stressful than enjoyable, and vowed to stick to subjects that wouldn't necessitate outright lying.

Clara had just begun to get comfortable when John took a sharp right-hand turn into what looked like a long driveway. She'd never been to this part of Harmony before, and wondered briefly if she were about to be taken to a secluded location, bashed over the head, and left for dead.

Okay, an unlikely scenario given her defensive capabilities, but that the notion sprang to her mind ahead of anything remotely romantic was something to think about later.

When the trees parted and she heard the sounds of bluegrass music wafting toward her, Clara let out a breath she hadn't known she'd been holding.

"Where are we?" She asked, raising an eyebrow and chancing a glance at John.

"Raylynn's B-B-Q," He replied with a smile, "She and her husband are southern transplants, and they brought their favorite recipes up here with them. They open during the summer months, and close when they run out of pulled pork. Tonight's the last of it. I hope you weren't expecting something fancier, but hole-in-the-wall is more my speed. Harmony's best-kept secret, in my humble opinion. Been coming here for years."

"I've never been much for fancy, so this is perfect. I'm just glad I didn't wear white." Clara could already detect the mouth-watering scents of simmering meat and barbecue sauce, and her sense of smell, honed from years working with herbs both fresh and dried told her it was homemade.

She let out a hum of appreciation, and her stomach rumbled.

From the outside, Raylynn's looked like a cobbled-together old country house, but inside it was comfortable and homey. The live band, made up of three elderly gentlemen, plucked away on their various acoustic stringed instruments, and for a second she almost believed they'd walked smack dab into the middle of the Deep South.

Sitting across from John, Clara tried to identify the sensations pinging around in her body. Some, the majority probably, came from plain old first date jitters—a mix of *he's looking at me* and *what if I say something stupid?*

There was also a hint of *what if he's hiding something to do with Brad.*

No. Tonight was just for her and for him. The mystery would have to take a backseat. Shoving suspicion firmly to the side, she let herself fall into the date without reservation.

John ordered for her, and while they dug into the food, she kept the conversation to superficial topics like books and movies.

"But why?" Clara asked, "This is why I despise horror movies. They always go back into the house, or the woods, or the abandoned factory. People that stupid deserve whatever happens to them. Give me a good, suspenseful ghost story any day."

"Not a fan of sappy romances?" John smiled.

Waving her fork at him, Clara pointed out, "See, right there you're showing your bias with the word sappy. Romance can be full of tragedy and comedy, too."

"Ah. The appeal of the brooding Heathcliff."

"Not my type, but I can see how he might seem romantic. I tend to go for the quirky leading man, myself. Less predictable."

John seemed to take that as a challenge, and pulling Clara from her seat, whirled her into his arms for a sprightly jig until the band took pity on him and played something softer and slower. He gathered her close and the scent of him flooded her senses.

Heart racing almost as fast as the previous song, Clara let herself float in the warmth she found in his arms. As first dates went, this one was shaping up nicely.

It ended at her front door with the breathless anticipation as his lips hovered over hers and she moved in to complete the kiss. Mingling her breath with his, she sighed when it ended, and wanted more.

"Good night, Clara Balefire. I'll see you soon."

She murmured a reply, and went to bed with a smile plastered to her face.

Chapter Eleven

Clara woke from a dream with the sounds of bluegrass music humming in her ears, and the memory of a kiss lingering on her lips. She absentmindedly dressed herself with a flicker of magic, and floated down the stairs to the shop on a cloud, only to find Mag waiting for her in the kitchen with a cup of coffee, smiling like the cat who ate the canary.

Pyewacket and Jinx were both, for once, in human form and seated rather than curled up in the other two chairs. "Clara and Jo-ohn, sittin' in a tree…" the three chorused. Clara found she didn't have it in her to be irritated and just rolled her eyes while pouring her own cup of coffee.

"So, how did it go? Of course, we were watching from the upstairs window, so we know how it ended." Mag waggled her eyebrows over the rim of her mug.

"It was great, actually. Except for the part where I can't tell him anything real about my life and who I am." The mere thought of it took some of the wind out of Clara's sails.

"You'll cross that bridge when you come to it. Worked for Mum and Papa. Course, those were different times, and the mere mention of witchcraft and magic didn't send people running for the hills." Clara had to give her sister credit, she was trying to be supportive.

"Maybe you're right."

"Maybe I am. What you need to do is drop your inhibitions and let things play out naturally," Mag stated with confidence.

"Since when did you become so well-versed in the nuances of witch-human relationships?" Clara wanted to know.

Mag plastered a haughty look on her face and stuck her nose in the air. "What you don't know about my past relationships could fill an entire novel, Clarie dear. Be nice, and maybe I'll tell you about them sometime."

"Ha, I'm betting it would take a whole bottle of Twinkleberry wine to pry those secrets out of you, and I'd rather not deal with the aftereffects, thank you very much." Clara retorted, the grin on her face stating clearly that she'd gladly nurse her sister's monster hangover if it meant finding out more details about the man who'd won Mag's heart back in the day. "Raincheck?"

"We'll see," Mag replied lightly, draining the last of her coffee. "Right now, I've got to take a ride over to Woodbridge and pick up some pieces I found in the Uncle Henry's. Jinx, I need manpower. Go hop in the VW."

Jinx scowled, but did as he was asked, leaving Clara to her own thoughts as she puttered around preparing the shop for the day's business.

Clara resisted the temptation to grab a daisy for a round of he'll call me/he'll call me not because she wasn't certain which outcome would suit her better. For a first date, it had gone remarkably well and that was a problem on so many levels. Not least, that he scared her spell-less.

Well, maybe he wouldn't call.

Of course, he would call. She was Clara Balefire, and not to be vain, but they almost always called.

This line of thinking persisted until the bell signaled her first customer of the day.

"Try this." A sample tube of soothing face cream dropped into a Balms and Bygones bag while Clara concentrated on presenting a reassuring smile. Not easy with the ghost of a young boy named Rydell hovering over the customer's shoulder. "Just the thing for repairing windburned skin, and if you put it on before you go out in the morning, it will provide a level of protection as well. I can tell you spend a lot of time outdoors."

With a cheerful grin and a nod, the forty-something woman pulled out a business card. "All four seasons. We offer guided horseback rides from our place in the valley below Pangborn Ridge. I love the horses and meeting new people, but the wind and sun do a number on the skin. Do you ride?"

At the mention of horses, the ghost spun like a whirlwind. "Ask her if the horses are gentle. And if they like apples or carrots better. Are their coats as soft as they look? I always wanted to touch one, but my doctor said it might mess up my immune system."

He pummeled her with a dozen more questions, which Clara ignored, but she tucked the woman's card into her pocket. Losing a battle with childhood cancer at age ten made Rydell's list of possible unfinished business a mile long and might include visiting a horse. Of all the ghosts hanging around, he was the one who haunted Clara the most. Not in the spooky way, but in the heartbreaking one.

"Not as often as I'd like," she replied to the woman. Pulling the card back out, Clara glanced at the name and address. Bells went off in her head. "You're Celia Pangborn? Like the ridge. You're not too far from Huffington Manor," she noted without surprise. In small towns, no one was ever too far from anyone else, geographically speaking. And how many Pangborns could there be in one small town? Celia must be related to Mason.

"Nope, not far at all, and I am Celia, like the ridge." A wistful smile replaced her cheerful one. "My brother and Kennedy Huffington grew up practically in each other's pockets, so Ken was in and out of our house for as long as I can remember. Such a tragedy, and now I hear there's another one. Poor Stephanie practically being left at the altar."

Fascinated, Clara subtly teased more information from Celia. Growing up, Stephanie's father preferred jeans and cowboy boots to khakis and loafers. He enjoyed a natural affinity with horses and would rather have studied to be a veterinarian than take on the Huffington legacy.

"Daddy used to joke that the storks mixed up those two babies on the way to Harmony because Mason hated anything to do with raising horses and they weren't too fond of him, either. Old Deacon tried to kick him through a wall once when we were teenagers. Broke three of Mason's ribs and gave him a concussion. Then again, Deacon didn't have much patience with humans except for Daddy and Ken. And truth be told, he only tolerated my father."

Once she got going, Celia could talk the paint off the wall.

Which led Clara to a dilemma. It seemed as if Celia might be a good source of information about John, but that would be prying and prying would be bad. Wouldn't it?

"What about John Masters? Were they friends back then, too?" So much for her resolve.

Besides, it couldn't be called prying with Celia so eager to talk. "John was a few years younger than Mase and Ken. Five or six, I think." Her eyes fluttered up and she frowned while she did the math. "Buffy was two grades behind me, and John was a year ahead of her, so that makes it five years."

Once she got going, Celia picked up the conversation and rolled along. "Yes, that's right. Mason was in his first year of law school when he helped John out of a little legal scrape."

"Even before he passed the bar? That's fascinating."

Tell me more, Clara thought.

"You ask me, it was Buffy got him into it, but John insisted the whole thing was his idea. John couldn't afford a lawyer, so Mason stepped in and coached him. You can represent yourself in court, though it's a stupid thing to do. It worked though—got it bargained down to petty theft, and because John wouldn't turn eighteen for another two months, they let him off with community service."

If there was more to learn, it would have to wait because Celia announced she'd be late if she didn't leave now, and reached for her bag of purchases.

"I have a party of five booked for an afternoon ride, and then I talked Mason into coming for dinner. He's been holed up in that office for the last two weeks, and I know he's not taking care of himself."

"I'm going with the horsey woman," Rydell called out, and dove into the bag as if it were a swimming pool.

"No, wait. You can't leave," Roma called out, but it was too late. Celia carried him out the door with no resistance whatsoever.

"Okay, I guess you can. Well, if he can do it." She zipped toward the door at full speed and rebounded in a cloud of ghostly essence. "Ouch. I guess it's just me."

"I'll be back," Mag said when the door closed behind Celia, leaving them alone in the shop.

"Where are you going?" The question fell into empty air because Mag was already gone.

Clara heaved a sigh and proceeded to throw herself into the familiar task of dusting in an attempt to quiet the pulsing thoughts occupying her brain. Of course, trying to ignore something usually just turned the volume up, and that was exactly what happened to Clara. It didn't help that she had an obnoxious elderly ghost peppering her with the very questions she wanted to ignore.

"What do you think he took? Says a lot about a man if he's willing to steal." As she zipped along near the ceiling, Roma's voice drifted down. "Maybe he's a bad egg. Could be he had something to do with Brad's disappearance. Do you think so? Should you go ask him some questions?"

Clara was about to start pulling her hair out by the roots. She vehemently wished there was some way to glean a little peace and quiet and a reprieve from the implications she wasn't yet ready to contemplate, but that she had every intention of contemplating anyway.

The image of John as a thief and a liar didn't gel with the impression she'd gotten after spending time with him. Was she blinded by her feelings for the man? He *had* hired a private investigator to look into Brad's past, but that didn't mean he would have resorted to running the man out of town or bashing him over the head with a paperweight.

Then Clara remembered the inkling she'd had the previous night when John had driven down that dirt road. Had it been her intuition, and if so, was she ignoring it because she was so attracted to him? Or, could she be over-thinking the whole thing because she *was* so attracted to him, and it scared the hell out of her?

All signs pointed to Brad having walked away of his own volition. It was only Stephanie's insistence that had kept the possibilities open, and all their investigating had only proved that Brad might have had multiple reasons for leaving town. Clara chose to hold onto that fact until there was evidence to the contrary, but Roma wouldn't stop trying to drive her opinions home.

"What are you going to do, Clara?" Roma sounded like a schoolyard bully, taunting her to the point where she was ready to snap.

Before Clara had a chance to blow her top, Mag sauntered through the door towing an irritated-looking Hagatha. The tennis balls on the feet of her walker thumped double-time as she tried to keep up.

"Look who I found wandering around the town square talking to herself." Mag said with an eye roll.

"She practically forced me into that death-mobile of yours, and insisted that my services were needed here. I'll have you know, my help doesn't come cheap, especially when I don't offer it willingly." Hagatha practically shouted, her conspicuous presence, or perhaps the well of power coiled deep inside her, calling all the ghosts into the front room of the store.

Clara quickly flicked a finger, flipping the sign on the door to 'closed' and closing the blinds to deter curious eyes and more customers. "Sorry, Haggie, but she's right. There's something weird going on here, and you're our only hope. We have need of your vast expertise." She laid it on thick, hoping to appeal to Hagatha's extended ego.

"Are you witches blind, or something?" Hagatha retorted, ignoring Clara's attempt at brown-nosing entirely. "Can't you see she's tethered? The rope is practically corporeal."

In return, Hagatha received a blank stare from both Balefire sisters as well as each and every ghost in attendance, including Roma.

"And you're supposed to be the best medium in the county." The accusation held less scorn than they would have been expected, since having a leg up on everyone around her was Hagatha's comfort zone, and she enjoyed lording her superiority enough to bring a smile to her deeply-lined face. "Follow me."

Hagatha made a beeline for the workspace behind the shop, following a trail nobody else could see. "There," She pronounced when Mag, Clara, and Roma filed in behind her, pointing toward the table where the crystal ball that had once been Roma's now sat.

"I still don't think any of us have any idea what you're talking about." Mag squinted, trying to see whatever it was Hagatha was seeing.

"Here, girl," Hagatha took off her spectacles and handed them to Mag, who didn't much like being referred to as 'girl' considering she was over two and a half centuries old, "Try now."

Mag slid the glasses onto her nose and looked around, her expression turning from bewilderment to understanding. She handed them to Clara, who repeated the experience minus the understanding part. Yes, she could see the glowing rope of energy, not unlike the filmy mist the ghosts were made of, except much brighter. But that didn't mean she had any clue what it meant or what to do about it.

"Why is she tied to that ball and how do we … um … free her?" Clara asked.

Mag cut Hagatha off before she could answer, causing the old witch to snatch her spectacles back and scowl.

"When I borrowed that thing," Mag pointed to the hunk of clear quartz crystal, "it was so full of Roma's essence I couldn't see anything clearly. I had to cleanse and recalibrate. I used Balefire, of course." She'd taken on her lecturing tone which meant she had some idea what had caused the problem.

"So?" Clara asked, her brow furrowed. "I don't see what that has to do with anything."

"It's simple cause and effect." Again with the lecture, only this time with patronizing overtones. "When Whizzer pushed Roma into the flames, the Balefire got a taste of her spirit. That's why it turned purple, the same color it turned when I cleared the ball."

"Clear as mud." Now Clara was annoyed.

"Two things in the house with the same flavor? Remember when Roma forgot she was dead and tried to touch the ball? That must have been enough to awaken any remnants of her energy, and when she fell into the fireplace, the Balefire reinforced the connection."

"It didn't just reinforce," Hagatha cut in, determined to add her two cents' worth, "It amplified. That's why she's stuck."

"And that's what drew the rest of the spirits, isn't it?" Clara wondered out loud. "Makes sense, I suppose. So now, what? We just have to break the connection? What would that entail?"

Hagatha grimaced, "An entire covens worth of spellwork, to start. Or ..." She glanced at Mag, who raised an eyebrow with suspicion. "You could take the easy way out and destroy the ball."

Mag puffed out her chest and raised her voice an octave. "Over my dead body are we destroying the most perfect specimen of a crystal ball I've ever seen. I'd rather—"

Before the rest of the group could find out what Mag would rather do, Roma let out a bellow. "I don't give a purple pony about your opinion, Margaret Balefire. That's *my* crystal, and therefore it's my choice. It's also *my* essence tied to it, and I'd like it back if you don't mind. Now, pick it up and do what you have to do. Or so help me, I'll stick around and irritate the socks off you for the next century, at least."

Mag looked from Roma to Clara to Hagatha, her eyes so full of frustration and misery Clara felt sorry for her even though Mag didn't have a leg to stand on. With an enormous sigh, she picked the crystal ball up off its pedestal and heaved it into the fireplace where it smashed into a million tiny shards.

Whatever it was—essence, energy, Mag didn't really care what it was called at that point—slammed back into Roma. She stiffened, the blurry edges of her ghostly form looking nearly solid for a moment.

"Here goes nothing," she shouted, and squeezed her eyes shut as if that would help. Floating at a decent speed, she hit the doorway and passed right through.

"It worked."

Three sets of human ears popped when a flood of ghosts streamed out of windows and doors. The mass exodus shook the foundation hard enough for dust to filter down from the cracks in the old plaster ceiling. A fine mist of ectoplasm swirled, then dissipated leaving only Roma, Kirk, and Whizzer behind.

Turning to Kirk, Mag demanded, "Why are you still here?" Too bad Whizzer couldn't answer that same question.

Ghost blushes might still come in shades of white or gray, but Kirk's was visible all the same. Keeping his face turned away from Clara, he admitted, "I thought maybe if I hung around long enough, I'd get a chance to see a naked woman. Or even a half-naked woman. I never had a girlfriend."

He might have thought he was playing the sympathy card, but as far as Clara was concerned, he was holding a dud hand. She opened her mouth to offer a tart reply, but Hagatha beat her to it.

"You'd like to see some boobies, eh?" The old witch grabbed the hem of her blouse and began to lift it to give Kirk a peek.

He emitted a yelp of protest, turned, and ran into the light as if the hounds of hell were on his tail. The last motes of him faded away to the sound of laughter.

"Guess he didn't want to see mine." Hagatha seemed a little disappointed.

Chapter Twelve

"Half-caff mocha latte!" Sebastian shouted, his eyes scanning the group of customers milling near the pick-up area. When nobody claimed the latte, he scrunched his eyebrows together in irritation and slammed it down, sloshing coffee out of the plastic lid and onto the counter. Without bothering to wipe up the spill, he turned his back and began making another order.

From her post at the register, Evelyn rolled her eyes and asked for Mag and Clara's order. "Kids these days, am I right?" she joked.

"You ain't kidding," Clara quipped back. "Just a mint tea and a cup of coffee, black."

"You got it." Evelyn pulled two to-go cups from a stack and shook her head in disgust. "Hey, *Bas*, go take a break." She tossed the suggestion over her shoulder, and Sebastian didn't waste any time disappearing out the side door.

She raised a brow at the sisters. "You don't happen to know anyone looking for a job, do you, Clara? I'd like to make some staffing changes, if you know what I mean."

Clara smiled. "I know all the same people you know, Evelyn. But I'll keep my ears open just in case. Say, how's your latest baking experiment going?"

"Actually," Evelyn replied with a sly grin, "I set one of the new donuts aside for you. I had a feeling you'd stop by today. Give it a try." She handed Clara what looked like a plain cake donut with a thick layer of milk chocolate glaze and some crushed bits of something amber-colored.

Whatever it turned out to be, it was sure to be delicious, and with that thought, Clara took a bite. "Oh! It's root beer!"

"Odd choice, I know," Evelyn grinned again, "but I happened to grab a root beer barrel out of the candy dish at the bank the other day, and inspiration struck."

Clara handed the other half of the creation to Mag, who took a closed-eyed nip and hummed with appreciation. "You have a gift, my dear. Passed down through the generations, it seems."

Evelyn beamed, "Thank you! Enjoy, and I'll see you two later." She greeted the next customer in line as the Balefire sisters made their exit.

Outside, around the corner from the front door, Sebastian was leaning against the exterior with one foot propped up against the wall behind him. A smartphone nearly the size of a tablet rested in one hand, and his thumb scrolled so fast Mag wondered how he could even register what he was looking at.

"Oh, hello there," he said when he noticed the Balefire sisters glancing his way. "Make any more progress on your investigation?" The word *investigation* came out with a sneer of derision that made Mag's blood boil. She had no patience for young people with no respect for their elders. She suspected *Bas* had no respect for anyone, including Cheyenne, but it wasn't her place to judge the bad taste of others. At least, not out loud.

He made a half-decent latte, she'd give him that much, but the attitude that came with it wasn't worth the price of the paper collar around the cup. Snark she could forgive. In fact, being Mag, she admired a good, pithy comeback. Sarcasm was her second language, but the line between it and just plain snotty was one he danced over with absolutely no grace whatsoever.

Worse, her estimation of Cheyenne dropped a notch for being such a bad judge of character when it came to choosing a boyfriend. Not that she'd thought much of the girl to begin with, but she wanted to believe, for Stephanie's sake, that Cheyenne's intentions were benevolent.

Clara may not have had more patience, but she had a better filter, so, shooting Mag a sideways glance, she quickly answered, "Not so far, but I'm sure we'll figure out what's going on eventually. We always do."

"You know you're just giving Stephanie false hope, don't you? What she needs is a dose of reality. Didn't it ever occur to her that Brad just wanted out? I mean, just because she's got money she thinks everyone should worship the ground she walks on. Typical snob." He spat the last word. "Money doesn't make her better or more important than anyone else."

Mag raised an eyebrow, but kept her cool, knowing it would be far more fun to watch him squirm if she remained calm, "It's interesting to me that you spend so much time worrying about something you claim not to care about. If you really want independence from society, why not go live off the land instead of peddling coffee and playing with your phone?"

Sebastian blanched, "Think what you want about Brad, but I saw him leave. At least *I* didn't just take off on my girlfriend out of the blue. Speaking of, here she comes."

One of Stephanie's town cars had pulled up to the curb while they'd been talking, and Cheyenne bounced out and over to Bas. She planted a lingering kiss on his lips, and even Clara was disturbed by the level of PDA going on in front of her.

"Hey ya'll, how's it going?" Cheyenne greeted the Balefires warmly, but Mag was too focused on what Bas had said right before she arrived.

"You saw Brad leave? Why didn't you say something before? Tell us what happened." Mag demanded.

Cheyenne's eyes widened, and she took a step back from Sebastian and repeated Mag's question. "I'd like to know the answer to that, myself. Why didn't you say anything?"

"I didn't think it made any difference." Bas's voice took on a whiny, somewhat contrite tone. "So what if he left in the morning or the middle of the night? He's still gone. Anyway, Cheyenne left something at my place and

I was dropping it off on my way to work. My day to work the early shift means I'm up and out by five, so it must have been quarter after by the time I got here."

"What else?" Cheyenne's temper was showing, and she stood with her arms crossed, glaring at Bas who grew more panicked by the second.

"I don't know, nothing really. I was going in, he was coming out, and in such a rush he practically mowed me over. I didn't think anything of it at the time. I said hey, he mumbled something and kept on going. That was the last I saw of the dude. I dropped Chey's handbag on the table, and just about made it to work on time."

And that was that. Proof that Brad had walked out the door under his own steam. Stephanie was not a killer, and Roma's unfinished business hadn't been much business at all.

Mag spent a solid minute imagining the exact color of fur she'd give Bas when she turned him into the jackass he'd already shown himself to be. He knew he was sitting on information that would have made a difference to Stephanie's state of mind, and he chose to do it anyway. She just hoped Cheyenne was smart enough to know that once a liar, always a liar.

"I can't believe you kept this to yourself. Just exactly what else are you hiding?" Cheyenne remained eerily calm, her emotions bubbling below the surface, making her seem even more formidable than if she'd been yelling and cursing.

"Nothing, baby, I swear!" Bas panicked, his eyes now the size of saucers, darting from Cheyenne over to

Mag and Clara as if looking for assistance. Both Balefire sisters held their hands up in a gesture indicating he was on his own, and took a step back to see how things played out.

Mag muttered under her breath to Clara, "This is better than reality TV." Clara heartily agreed.

"Don't 'baby' me, Bas. In fact, don't ever call me that again. I'm not your baby anymore."

"But, wait, Chey, come on. It's not like I lied to you, I just didn't say anything. Please, don't do this to me." Bas sputtered, and Mag wished she had a bucket of popcorn.

"It's called a lie by omission, *Sebastian*, and it still falls under the umbrella of dishonesty. Now, maybe if what you had failed to mention was that you were the one who used the last of the toilet paper, I could get past it. But what you did do was leave out vital information, and to me that feels like an outright lie. You hurt Stephanie, which means you hurt me, and I won't stand for either." Cheyenne spun on her heel and stalked back over to the town car.

"Mag, Clara, why don't you follow me up to the manor." She tossed behind her. "Brad needs to get back to his *brew steward* duties. That is, if he still has a job."

Clara thought the odds of that were doubtful, since every one of Evelyn's customers—and the lady herself— were staring out the front window as if this really were reality television. She caught Evelyn's eye and smirked, then followed Cheyenne's lead and left Bas standing on the sidewalk, a priceless expression on his face.

Chapter Thirteen

Normally unruffled, Constance looked ten years older when Mag, Clara, and Cheyenne walked through the door. When she lifted a hand to push back hair she hadn't bothered to put in her usual neat bun, her fingers trembled. Wrinkles in her dress, the collar sticking up on one side, all spoke of a woman in some distress.

"I promise we won't take up too much of Stephanie's time. This has to be hard on her, not knowing where Brad went, and it can't be easy for you to watch her struggle through this. Is there anything we can do for you?"

The offer, or the kindness behind it, sparked a reaction from Constance. Turning, she let the mask of polite service fall to show the weariness underneath. "Find out what happened and give my girl some peace. It's all I ask."

Sympathy oozing from every pore, Clara patted Constance on the shoulder and agreed to do just that as the sound of violin music filled the house. Each note vibrated with heartbreaking purity and Clara's breath caught in an ache at the back of her throat. How could something sound so beautiful and haunting at the same time?

Stephanie sat on a piano stool, her back straight and strong, yet somehow fragile as she played. When the last note drifted into silence, she turned and placed the violin back in its case before looking at her guests.

"That was lovely. You have a gift." Even the mighty Mag was not so heartless that she didn't felt a little choked up.

"Thank you." she stated, then raised an eyebrow in an expectant gesture. Clara remembered Roma's comment about Stephanie possessing '*the* gift' and wondered if the woman could tell they weren't making a social call.

Cheyenne launched into an animated retelling of her breakup with Bas. The part where she mimed his expression when she'd left him standing, at a loss, in front of Evelyn's Bakery brought a shadow of a smile to Stephanie's face. The tale ended with, "It all comes back to what happened that morning to send Brad out so early. If we had that, we'd have the whole story."

"She was amazing," Mag said gazing at Cheyenne with newfound respect, "and it was hilarious watching him try to figure out what had just happened."

"Good riddance, is what I say. Cheyenne, you could do far better than that arrogant knob." Constance, as usual, minced no words.

Cheyenne bristled slightly, in the way most women do when their taste in men is questioned by, essentially, two little old ladies. "He had his good qualities, you know. And he ..." Cheyenne trailed off and mumbled something that sounded like *troubled childhood.*

During all of this, Stephanie's face ran through a gamut of emotions. Relief that Brad had been alive and well when he left that morning, and therefore she couldn't have had anything to do with his disappearance. Fear that she'd been wrong all along and that Brad actually did leave because he didn't really love her. And finally, misery at the thought that for her, it was a no-win situation. Dead, done, or on the run—none of the options brought a smile to Stephanie's face.

Clara felt the waves of tension rolling off Stephanie and sent a tendril of intuition to test the flavor. "Stephanie Huffington. You stop thinking that way right now." The exclamation came out of the blue for everyone who wasn't Stephanie or Clara.

"There is still hope, but you're going to have to woman up and think positively. *I'm* positive that you're strong enough to do that. Are you?" Clara demanded.

Stephanie gathered herself together, sat up a little straighter, and looked Clara in the eye. "Yes. I am. What I'm not is certain I have any idea what to do from here."

"If only we knew what happened between the time he went to bed and the time he jumped in his car and took off." Cheyenne repeated her earlier statement.

Stephanie shook her head. "Oh, but he didn't get in his car and leave because it wasn't here at the time."

The picture forming in Mag's head shifted like a kaleidoscope and settled into a new configuration of scenarios that she let run rampant for a moment.

"Where's the car now?"

"I assume it's still over at Malverde's garage. We'd dropped it off there for its yearly service and detailing and I forgot all about it with everything that's happened."

A little spark of discovery fired, and took the energy level in the room up a notch. There was something here, a detail that might make all the difference. "Did he get a loaner? Use your car? Ride a bike? It's a long walk from here to town."

Pausing for a moment, Stephanie considered. "At that time of day he'd have caught a ride with Pete Barber. Pete lives a mile or so down the road, and milks cows over at Willow Hill farm. He's dependable as the tides and comes through here at the same time every morning. That's brilliant thinking, Mag."

Accepting the compliment as nothing less than her rightful due, Mag barely preened at all. "That would explain why he was in such a hurry to get out the door when Bas saw him. And now we have a new line to tug."

"You're going to have to tug it without me, because I have a class to get to," Cheyenne lamented. "I wish I could skip it, but there's an exam today. Promise you'll text me if you find out anything useful?" She kissed Stephanie's cheek on her way out, a little spring in her step.

About a mile down the road, just as Stephanie had described, sat a little farmhouse that looked like it dated back at least a hundred years. Rows of meandering pumpkin plants had been picked clean, with only a few oddly shaped stragglers left over from jack-o-lantern season. The grounds appeared well-kept, as did the house, though it needed a bit of work and could have used a fresh coat of paint to cover the spots where the siding showed bare wood.

Pete Barber's eyes goggled about out of his head when he opened the door to find Stephanie standing on his stoop flanked by Mag and Clara, who made an interesting pair all on their own.

"Come on in. Is everything all right, Steph?" Mag noted the familiarity with which he spoke to Stephanie, his attitude at odds with most of the people in town who thought of the girl as nothing more than a symbol of wealth and the power that came with it.

Mag appreciated the fact that Stephanie's personal relationships were few and far between—it was a trait they both shared—and reserved for the folks who could look past the status and see the smart, compassionate woman underneath. She immediately liked Pete Barber just based on that principle alone, and her gut screamed they were getting closer to solving the mystery.

"Actually, it's not, and I need you to answer a few questions for us, if you don't mind." Stephanie replied. "These are my friends, Mag and Clara." She gave no further explanation for their presence, and Pete didn't ask for any.

"Sure, sure. Come on in." Pete led them through a narrow hallway and into a small country living room where he offered them a seat on a sofa that Mag suspected dated back to when the house was built. When she sat down between Clara and Stephanie, one of the springs poked straight into her backside, causing her to scoot a bit closer to her sister. "What's going on?"

"Well, there's no easy way to say this, but Brad's gone missing." Stephanie explained. "We suspect foul play of some kind, and I need you to tell me everything about the last time you saw him. You gave him a ride into town last week, right?"

Pete looked back and forth between the trio and nodded. "Last Wednesday morning, yes, that's correct."

"That's the day he disappeared. Tell me what happened and don't leave anything out. It's important," Stephanie implored.

"Well, there's not much to tell, really." Pete's eyes drifted to one side, and Mag's opinion of him as one of the good guys took a bit of a beating. Dollars to donuts, he planned on holding something back, and she intended to find out exactly what it was.

"He flagged me down on my way to work and I'll admit it didn't look like he'd slept a wink. Asked could I drop him off in town, even though I told him it was no problem to swing by Pets Alive if he needed to get to work," Pete explained.

"Where exactly did you drop him?" Mag opened her mouth to ask, but Stephanie beat her to it.

"Right in the square. He hustled out of my truck so fast, I didn't have time to see if he needed me to wait for him. But he said he had to talk to your uncle." Another shifty eye caught Stephanie's attention this time.

"What aren't you saying, Pete? I've known you my entire life, so there's no need to beat around the bush." She pierced him with a gaze that explained at least part of why people tended to walk on eggshells around Stephanie. The woman could be formidable when necessary.

Pete sighed and gave in. "Well, I wasn't in a mood myself, and spent most of the drive complaining about the dismal pumpkin sales we'd been seeing. Christine's been working double shifts at the hospital just so we can get by, and that money was supposed to go toward getting the house fixed up."

He waved a hand to indicate the state of the interior. "You know she's been dying to redo the living room, and we've been saving to replace the old wood siding with vinyl. Anyway, we had that drought and then all that rain, and to top it all off there were more drive-offs than usual this year."

Clara gave Mag a look. They'd had some part in the weather trouble over the summer, and now she felt bad.

"We expect to lose some profits since we can't be right here to cash people out, but this year it was worse than ever. I said something about how small-town life was going down the toilet, and Brad responded with something like 'people are rarely who you think they are'." He couldn't meet Stephanie's eyes, and it was clear Pete had taken Brad's statement as a slam against Stephanie.

"I figured maybe the two of you had a fight, and I didn't want to pry." He finished lamely.

"We didn't have a fight. That's what I can't understand." Stephanie was quiet for a moment. "Was there anything else that seemed off to you? Any detail might be critical."

Pete thought for a second before answering. "No, not really. I remember feeling sorry for him. When he walked away across the square, he looked angry and hurt. His fists were clenched, and the thought crossed my mind that I wouldn't want to be on the other end of them that morning. I know that doesn't help much. He gave me money for gas, and I felt low taking it, but he insisted."

"You've been a big help, actually. Thanks, Pete. I appreciate you talking to us. Now, I'll call them and give permission for you to use my account the hardware store. You haven't got much time left to get that siding up, and combined with my discount, you'll save half the cost just in heating bills this winter. You can start paying me back if the pumpkin crop is good next season."

When he started to protest, she added, "I mean it, Pete. I'll just have them send the materials over myself if you don't, and I'll choose the ugliest color they have." She threatened with a smile. "I think of you like family, so you'll let me do this for you."

"You're a classy dame, Stephanie Huffington." Pete said gruffly as the three women exited. Neither Mag nor Clara could disagree with the sentiment.

"I need to call Uncle John." Stephanie stated on the ride back to Huffington Manor. "He's got some explaining to do."

Clara heartily agreed, and her heart skipped a beat at the mention of John. The thought that he might have held something back from Stephanie didn't sit well with her, and combined with what she'd learned from Celia, her intuition was starting to chirp.

She wasn't sure if Stephanie knew about the date, but before she had a chance to say anything on the subject, Roma popped into the back of Stephanie's town car and the temperature dropped ten degrees.

"Sorry about that. I'm still getting use to this whole ghost thing." She apologized with one of her trilling laughs. When no one rushed to assure her it was fine, she said, "What am I? Invisible?"

Clara had to nod toward Stephanie before Roma caught on. "Oh, right."

Chapter Fourteen

"Someone's coming," Roma warned about a half a second before Constance ushered Mason into the room, and when Mag muttered something snarky at her, the response set the housekeeper off on a search for the cold draft.

"Sorry." Roma retreated to a corner to reduce her chilling effect on the living.

Clara rated a fleeting once-over from the new arrival before he turned his attention to Stephanie. "Sorry to show up unannounced, but I was out this way and I have those papers you wanted. The business agreements for the funds for Cheyenne. I just need you to sign on a few dotted lines and I'll be on my way."

While a delighted Stephanie scanned and signed each document, Mason sat quietly. Though his gaze kept straying toward Clara, he made no effort at engaging in small talk. As she handed each paper over, he carefully replaced it in the folder and waited for the next.

When she was finished, he offered a half-hearted congratulations on the new venture, and asked if there was any news from Brad.

When she said there wasn't, he replied, "I'll draw up the dissolution of agreement for Pets Alive this week."

Aghast at the suggestion, Stephanie vehemently disagreed. "Why on earth would you do a thing like that? There are still animals in need of assistance, are there not? I wasn't funding the program because my fiancé was director. Honestly, Mason. You're getting to be as bad as Uncle John with the purse strings."

"I thought, well, never mind what I thought."

Clara's phone interrupted whatever Mason might have said next, and she didn't need to see Winifred's number on the screen to know the call was important. The intuitive chill that ran from her gut down to her toes did that quite nicely, and had nothing to do with Roma's presence.

Clara's half of the conversation consisted of a few yeses and an okay, we'll be right there.

She hung up, noticed the sea of expectant faces, and struggled with a dilemma. Should she just drag Mag out of there with some flimsy excuse, or tell Stephanie the news right now?

Best to go with the truth.

"That was Winifred from Pets Alive. Someone found Brad's wallet, saw his business card inside, and figured he'd drop it off there instead of the police station. Winifred is holding it for us, and thought it best we break the news to Stephanie ourselves." Clara explained.

"What do you think this means?" Pale, but holding herself together, Stephanie asked.

Mason answered before Clara could. "I think it proves Brad wasn't the man you thought he was. He's probably living it up somewhere under an assumed name."

"If he didn't want to get married, he could have asked for the ring back, and I'd have given it to him. I think changing his identity takes breaking up to a bit of an extreme, don't you?"

It looked like Mason might argue the point, but he chose to go, and to leave Clara wondering why he didn't tell Stephanie he was investigating possible misuse of the shelter funds. She'd have liked to ask him if he'd found anything, but she never had the chance.

"We'll scoot over and pick it up, and come right back." Clara promised, leaving Stephanie in Constance's care.

Ten minutes later, with Mag at the wheel, Clara declared, "This changes things."

Mag considered all the possible ramifications and none of them landed on a best case scenario. "It sure does."

When they arrived at the shelter, Winifred explained how Brad's wallet had been found on a roadside embankment heading north on the way out of town. The man who found it was from Port Harbor, and hadn't realized how close he was to Harmony and a restroom when nature's call became too persistent to ignore. He'd been looking for a secluded spot to relieve himself when he stumbled upon the wallet, and decided to do the decent thing and attempt to return it. Finding Brad's business card tucked inside, he dropped the wallet at the shelter.

"There's money in it," Winifred said as she handed over the wallet. "This whole things seems a bit fishy to me.

My intuition is screaming." She spoke the last sentiment in a hushed, conspiratorial tone.

Clara couldn't help but agree. "Thanks so much, Winifred. We'll take it from here, and we'll keep you in the loop." She could scarcely believe that of all people, one of Penelope Starr's henchwomen had finally conceded that the Balefire sisters were worthy of this level of trust. It was about time, and maybe it meant they were making headway in the coven. Clara vehemently hoped so, because being at odds with the people she was supposed to trust had taken a toll.

"Ha, I told you there was danger, and this proves it beyond a shadow of a doubt!" Appearing out of thin air, Roma hovered over the rear seat and gloated.

Mag's blood pressure rose by a few points. "We haven't proven anything yet, Roma. Don't get your panties in a knot before we have more information."

Roma blew a raspberry in Mag's direction, "Ghosts don't wear panties. At least, I don't think."

Mag scowled at her. "That wasn't really the point. This is serious."

Clara slapped the wallet into Mag's waiting hand while Roma poked her head in between the seats for a better look.

Sure enough, there was over one hundred dollars in the billfold, several credit cards and a debit card, his driver's license, and a photo of Stephanie tucked inside.

Mag's nose twitched and she raised the wallet to her face and took a big sniff. "There's blood trace on the leather." She said with certainty. "Just a drop or two."

"How on earth do you do that?" Clara asked, having observed Mag's senses at work before, when they had been involved in another murder investigation.

"Years of practice. Blood leaves a metallic scent, and a sort of aura to the trained eye." Mag was more than proud of the abilities she'd honed over the years, but not in any huge rush to fill her little sister in on the events that had made it necessary to cultivate such a skill.

If Clara had an inclination that Mag felt that way, it would have made her blood boil. They hadn't been kids for over two centuries, and while Mag's protective nature was sweet and all, it was also downright irritating.

"Like I said," Roma gloated, "Danger."

"Trouble is," Mag continued, "There's no definitive way to prove it's Brad's blood. But something tells me Stephanie isn't going to take that nuance into consideration, and I can't say I blame her. It looks bad."

"Don't tell her about the blood. What could it possibly help?" As Clara pulled back onto the main road, Roma threw her opinion into the mix and started an argument with Mag that lasted the whole way back to Huffington Manor and required her to turn the heat up to compensate for the chill.

They found Stephanie pacing the garden nervously, and to stop any further comments from the peanut gallery, Clara took the lead. She showed Stephanie the wallet and broke the news as gently as she could. "I'm sorry, but we've discovered something and I don't want you to panic."

"When someone says not to panic, it usually means that's exactly what you ought to do," Stephanie commented dryly. "Hit me."

"It doesn't look like it was stolen because the contents appear intact, but we there appears to be blood trace on the leather," Clara said, laying it on the table.

Stephanie's face crumpled, along with her put-together facade. Clara knew exactly where her mind had gone—straight to, of course, the most horrific possible conclusion—that Brad was dead. She couldn't help but think the poor woman might be right.

"Now I wish he really had just left me. That would be better."

Clara wrapped her arms around Stephanie in a show of comfort. "There's still no body, and it's possible the blood wasn't even Brad's. There's still hope."

"Not for me." Stephanie lamented, marching back into the house where a newly returned Cheyenne was tucking into a chicken salad sandwich while Constance puttered around making yet another pot of tea.

"Constance, call the police. Tell them I'm ready to turn myself in." Eerily composed, Stephanie gave the order. Convinced of his death from the beginning, it was as if finding proof let her gather the shattered bits of her grief into a numbing ball of calm at her center.

Pandemonium erupted with Cheyenne and Constance shouting down the idea until Mag put her fingers in her mouth and let out a piercing whistle. "No one is calling the police until a body turns up."

Leave it to Mag to say the least sensitive thing in any situation. Neither tact nor diplomacy came easy to her, though she could access both if she wanted to. She rarely did.

"What my sister meant to say"—Clara pinned Mag with a stern look—"was, let's not get hasty until we've examined all the facts. First of all, we now know Brad left the house in the morning, not in the middle of the night, and he was upset about something. That changes everything."

Her face becoming more remote by the second, Stephanie said, "It changes nothing. I watch him die every night in my dreams." And now Clara worried what had looked like calm might be shock. It was time to pull Stephanie back to reality.

"Did you and Brad have a fight the night before he disappeared?" Tone sharp, Clara whipped out the question and snapped her fingers to hurry the answer. It was the same trick she'd used on Harold's ghost.

"No."

"Were you cheating on Brad?"

"No." Finally, some fire bled back into Stephanie's eyes.

"Would he cheat on you?"

"No. And I resent—"

"Were you on good terms with him when you went to sleep?"

"Yes."

A few more questions later, Clara hit her with the money shot.

"Did you kill Bradley Graham with a paperweight?"

"No, I didn't."

Stephanie was the only one in the room who seemed surprised by the admission.

"Good, I didn't think so," Clara said, brushing off her hands. "Now, we can get on with figuring out what happened to him."

The front door of Stephanie's house closed with a loud bang, and John burst into the library where the three women (and one currently invisible ghost) were gathered.

"What's going on? Is everything all right?" He asked, his eyes skimming over Clara completely in his haste to find out why his niece had sent a 9-1-1 message. "I was in a meeting, and my cell was off."

Stephanie allowed herself to be swept up in a concerned hug. "I'm sorry, I didn't mean to scare you, but we needed to speak to you as soon as possible." She recapped the conversation with Pete and the discovery of the wallet once John had greeted Mag and Clara and taken a seat around the coffee table.

"I wish I could say I'd seen him that morning, but I didn't. I had a breakfast meeting and didn't get to the office until almost ten-thirty. Did Pete say what it was Brad wanted to talk to me about?" John's eyebrow quirked when he asked, and his foot tapped the floor while he waited for Stephanie to answer.

She sighed. "No, he didn't. I was hoping you'd have some idea."

John's face clouded over. "I wish I had a different answer for you, but I don't. Do you think it might be time to put this to rest? It looks pretty cut-and-dried to me. I know it hurts when someone doesn't feel the same way about you as you do about them, but the best thing to do is move on. You're a beautiful, generous woman, and you deserve someone who can see that for himself."

Stephanie's eyes welled with tears, and Clara could sense sadness, anger, and frustration rolling off her in waves. Mag felt it too, and was more than mildly curious to find out what might happen if Stephanie threw Miss Manners' book of etiquette out the window and actually said what she was feeling for once.

"Thank you, Uncle John. I'll take that into consideration." Mag was sorely disappointed when Stephanie tamped down her reply, turned her back on the room, and stared out the window with her arms crossed.

John held up his hands in surrender and bowed his head. "I guess I'll leave you ladies alone." He shot a pointed look in Clara's direction.

"I'll walk you out." Clara offered, following him to the door.

When they were alone, John's shoulders slumped even further. "I don't know what else to do. I feel just as helpless as I did when her parents died. It practically killed Buffy too, but we had to be strong for Steph. I'm glad you and your mother are here for her; it means a lot, and she could use some female attention."

"We're happy to help," Clara replied. She couldn't put her finger on why, but all her lovely, warm feelings for him had evaporated during the walk from the sitting room to the door.

While she tried to figure out why, she lost track of the conversation. "—Friday night?"

"I'm sorry, what?"

"I was asking you out, and apparently not doing a very good job of it."

"Can I get back to you on that? I think there's something … I need to check my schedule. I'll call you, okay?" She couldn't say yes until she'd had time to explore her sudden ambivalence to him. "I'm sorry. There's a lot going on, and I think Stephanie needs me."

The confusion on his face mirrored her emotional state, but she turned and went back inside, anyway.

Things were in quite a state when Clara returned to the library. Roma whizzed overhead, her edges blurring as her excitement notched up another level.

"We've got another lead." Roma exclaimed.

"We've got another lead." Stephanie had no idea she was repeating Roma's statement. "Maybe not a lead, but it's something. I remembered Pete said Brad's fists were clenched at his sides when he walked away from his truck. That means he wasn't holding onto his briefcase, and that is one thing he would never leave behind."

Still caught up in whatever had just happened with John, Clara tried to focus.

"I've already called Pete, and he confirmed Brad wasn't carrying anything when he picked him up, but he was poring over those files all evening before I fell asleep that night. They weren't on his bedside table, and I haven't seen them since. Those files might be the key to what happened to him, or at least give us a clue. We've got to find them!"

"It's something," Mag allowed, "Let's split up and look for them. Maybe we can get Constance to help. She knows this place far better than Clara or I do."

"Can't you just, I don't know, conjure Brad's briefcase to your hand?" Stephanie asked.

In the interest of saving time that would be spent listening to one of Mag's diatribes about how magic worked, Clara answered for her sister.

"It doesn't work that way. We have to know where an object is before we can call it to us. Even if it were that simple, we wouldn't be able to tell where it had come from, and Brad's hiding place might have some significance."

Stephanie accepted Clara's explanation and called in Constance, who jumped on board immediately and agreed to help look for the files Brad had been working on the night he disappeared.

"You two start in the bedroom and search the upstairs. Constance and I will take the bottom floor." Mag suggested.

An hour later, after every nook and cranny in the downstairs had been explored, Mag made painful progress up the stairs to spend another hour helping continue the search.

"Try to think like Brad," she offered helpfully. "Where would he hide the briefcase?"

Looking more disheveled than Mag had seen her, Stephanie threw herself backwards on the bed and offered a tart reply. "Why thank you; I'd have never thought of that on my own." The snark warmed Mag's heart and gave her hope.

"He's a man. Men are a lot like children, they tend to shove things under the furniture."

"First place we looked." Clara swiped her forearm across her forehead to clear the sheet of sweat.

"Found it." Roma sang out. "Top of the wardrobe, hidden behind the decorative trim. It was the mention of kids that made me look. If they're not hiding things under the furniture, they go for on top."

A sound piece of logic which Clara parroted when, as the tallest of the two Balefires, she reached a questing hand past the molding, and triumphantly pulled out the briefcase. "Found it," she sang, and handed it to Stephanie.

"I'm nervous to see what's inside. This could be the key to everything." A tentative finger pressed the latch. "It's locked."

"Because that would be too easy."

With Constance downstairs, and safely out of sight, Mag used magic to pop the lock, and then came the moment of truth.

Taking a deep breath, Stephanie opened the briefcase and pulled out a stack of manila folders. She fell silent as she leafed through the files, and then frowned.

"These have nothing to do with the shelter," She noted, surprised. "They're records from Huffington Foundation."

Mag shot a sharp glance in Clara's direction. The question of whether he'd been plotting some nefarious plan to siphon funds from Pets Alive had been answered, but now Mag's suspicion that he'd been attempting to swindle money out of Stephanie rose to the top of the list of possibilities. What other reason he might have had to be delving into her finances was quickly answered as Stephanie put her Yale MBA to use.

"You've got to be kidding me." She stated, shuffling papers back and forth and paying special attention to the sections Brad had highlighted. "Someone has been siphoning money out of the foundation, and it looks like Brad found out about it."

Clara's heart dropped into her stomach. Brad had made the discovery and headed straight to speak to John. John had control over the foundation, which gave him the opportunity and means. The motive wasn't hard to discern; the adage that money made the world go 'round had been proven true more times than a calculator could compute.

"Who had access to the funds in question?" Clara asked, praying to the Goddess there was some other explanation.

"Me, obviously, but I think we can rule me out for obvious reasons. Uncle John, Mason, the head accountant. I've been taking a more active role, but Uncle John still oversees the day-to-day operations, which includes bookkeeping and accounting."

She paused for a breath, then continued speaking while her gaze scanned more of the pages. "Mason handles all our legal needs, but there's a fair amount of overlap between them because as our tax attorney, he also advises on financial matters and is active in handling our investments. There's a bookkeeper who sets up some of the payments, but one of the three of us signs the checks. Not that anyone uses checks anymore, but you know what I mean."

Any further speculation ceased when Constance marched into the room. "It's time for dinner. Now you clean yourselves up and come downstairs, and I won't have any more talk of this at the table. Stephanie needs to keep up her strength for whatever is to come."

"We should be leaving." Mag tried to beg off from a dinner spent under the baleful eye of Constance counting the silver, but Clara couldn't ignore the niggling feeling she was needed here.

"I think we should stay and keep Stephanie company this evening. She might have need of our *special talents* while she sorts things out."

"And I have a shipment to unpack. We do have a shop to run." Mostly, Mag had hit her limit of being social for the day.

Picking up on the meaning of the term *special talents*, Stephanie turned to Clara. "There are plenty of extra bedrooms. Why don't you stay the night and let Mag go home and handle things there."

That was logic Mag couldn't and didn't want to dispute, so off she went for her first night alone in months.

Chapter Fifteen

Feeling no remorse whatsoever, Mag tore through Clara's kitchen looking for the bottle of faerie-made wine she knew was hiding somewhere in the cupboards. The Fae had a reputation for luring humans into their homes and plying them with food and drink in order to trap them there for a thousand years.

The thousand years part was so much hooey, Mag thought, but she'd never yet met the human who could drink more than half a glass of the potent Twinkleberry wine and not lose a solid week or more to its heady intoxication.

The magic blood coursing through her veins could handle the effects far better than a regular human, but if it didn't and she had to choose a week to lose, though, this one was currently at the top of her list. If she never saw another ghost, it would suit her just fine.

The wine turned up in the hallway, stuffed into one of Clara's old boots. Clearly, she hadn't wanted it found. Well that was just too bad for Clara. Mag popped the cork with a look, took the first swig right from the bottle, and prepared to enjoy her first night alone in more months than she cared to remember.

No matter how much she enjoyed the quality time with her sister, a body needed some peace every once in a while. A little space to breathe, to cut loose. Pyewacket had taken herself off to Port Harbor for the night, Roma was with Clara, and if the ghosts knew what was good for them, they'd keep to their own plane of existence.

Tiny bubbles floated out of the pink liquid and rang like little bells when they popped. Closing her eyes, Mag tipped the bottle up again and the second sip buzzed a path down to her toes. Glasses were for sissies.

Home alone, completely free. She should head back over to her place and fire up the old Crosley unit she'd pilfered from the shop along with a box of vintage vinyl. About ten steps toward the door, she realized she was too wobbly to navigate the stairs.

Witch perk, she thought, as she conjured the suitcase-style record player from her closet and it landed on Clara's kitchen table with a thump. A few things from the shop would make this a party. Another short draw on the bottle stole a little more of her concentration, but not so much that she couldn't summon a little mood lighting for the party.

Mag's decorating tastes ran straight Victorian, all the way, but when it came time to cut loose and have a little fun, she partied like it was 1969. Or at least the decade between sock hops and disco.

With a little frown of concentration wrinkling her forehead, she chose a nice lava lamp and a disco ball from the contents of her shop, and settled them into place with a nice, steady flow of magic.

She programmed the Balefire colors to add a little more ambiance, and settled down to enjoy the peace.

Except the peace was a little too peaceful.

"Bored now." Mag commented to the empty room. "Hagatha Crow. Hagatha Crow. Hagatha Crow."

Comparing Hagatha to Beetlejuice or Bloody Mary tickled Mag's sense of humor and she didn't expect calling her name three times to work. When it did, her mind was too muddled to follow through on the implications.

"Care for a snort?" The bottle, when she handed it over, was still three-quarters full even if Mag looked like she was four days in on a three-day bender.

"Well, well. Someone has been using their Faerie connections." Lifting the bottle to her nose, Hagatha inhaled, sneezed when a few bubbles tickled, then toasted Mag and took a healthy drink. A stray moment of clarity made Mag think lowering Hagatha's inhibitions might be a bad idea, but in the interests of not being drunk alone, she waved it away.

Taking turns, they put a hurt on the better part of the bottle and began trading stories from past exploits, including the one that ended with the Raythe that drained away Mag's youth.

"See, it wasn't a spell," Mag slurred, watching the Balefire flames dance, "so Clara's barking up the wrong tree thinking she can find a way to fix me. I'm not fixable."

"Unicorn feathers!" Hagatha snorted. "Magical being did the deed, that's enough."

While Mag's mind went off on a wild tangent and tried to picture a unicorn because her muddled brain couldn't remember whether they had feathers or not, her drinking companion listed off a combination of spells that, woven together, might work.

"Complicated one, that spell. And then you'd need a—," Hagatha flapped her hand while she searched for the right words. "Hair of the dog. Raythe blood or bone would work. Too bad you lost all that pixie honey. It would take most of a hive's worth to distill enough hormones."

Squinting, Mag tried to take it all in. Could there really be a way to regain her lost youth? Or was Hagatha just blowing faerie dust out of her behind? In the pink twilight of her wine-induced haze, Mag thought it sounded plausible, but then again, she also thought she could hear her hair growing, so who knew?

Clara stared out into the icy depths of the howling snowstorm, a violent shiver playing down her spine while she tried to make out shapes through the unrelenting white. Everything before this moment was a blur, and she couldn't remember how or why she'd come to be in this place, freezing to death.

She spun in place, trying to decide which direction to take when everything looked the same. Tendrils of dread inched down her body to grow the kind of roots that bound a person's feet to the ground.

Tension built to the point where biting down on the scream wouldn't be enough to hold it back, and she opened her mouth to let it fly.

"Clara Balefire. You wake up now!" Steam wafted when Roma's ice met Clara's warm breath. "Something is wrong and you need to wake up."

"What?" Bleary eyes crusted with sleep and ghost chill, Clara finally surfaced to find Roma's prone figure hovering about an inch above her. "Get off me, and quit breathing in my face."

Another cold gust blew past Clara's face as Roma huffed in frustration. "Wake up and listen, you daft witch. Someone is prowling around downstairs. Now, you need to get out of that bed, and go check on Stephanie. Right this minute. Do you hear me?"

"I don't … what?"

"Someone. Is. In. The. House." More puffs of chilled air blew tossed Clara's hair and she finally tuned into what Roma had said. "My danger alarms are blaring."

"Stephanie."

Shedding sheets and blankets like a cocoon, Clara rose and dressed herself with magic. Three long steps took her to the door as her hair bound itself out of her eyes, and then she turned back to look for her magically miniaturized bag of tricks.

Precious seconds went into figuring out it wasn't there and trying to remember why.

"Where? How many?" Voice pitched low, Clara decided she'd have to make do with only the magic her mama gave her.

"One and I'm not sure where he is now, since you took your sweet time waking up."

"Dial back the cranky. I'm up now." All the way up, and fueled with enough adrenaline to make her fingers feel shaky when she eased the door open and pressed her ear to the crack.

Was that a stealthy footstep, or just her own pulse fluttering in her ear?

"Oh for Pete's sake." Roma's voice ricocheted off the walls with a distant, hollow-sounding echo and startled Clara hard enough to draw a flicker of Balefire into the palm of her hand. She doused the flames, but not before they compromised her night vision.

If Roma weren't already dead, Clara would have been tempted to send the medium into the light with her butt on fire. "I hope whoever it is can't hear you," she stepped away from the door and whispered.

"If I thought he could, I'd put the fear of Roma into him. Wait here." With that, Roma swept through the door, presumably to go locate the intruder.

Clara did wait. Not because Roma told her to, but because she needed a moment to prepare herself for what was to come. The angel on her shoulder insisted it could not be John sneaking around the house with murky intentions. The devil on the other figured he was as good a suspect as any. Heaven help him if it was, because that would put two marks against him in her book.

Worse, for Stephanie's sake, would be the ultimate betrayal if Brad had returned like a thief in the night.

"What are you waiting for? Go protect Stephanie." In the darkness, Roma looked like a pale shadow.

Wait, don't wait. Roma needed to make up her mind. "Where is he? Did you see who it is?" Clara asked.

"Ransacking the office, so why are you just standing there? If he hurts her, I swear I'll haunt you forever."

"Go to Mag, tell her what's happening, and get her to call the cops before she does anything else. I'll take care of Stephanie."

Keeping that promise would take all her concentration, and getting rid of Roma's distracting influence was half the goal with sending her for help. "Go now!"

Whether it was stealthy footsteps or merely the sound of her own pulse whooshing in her ears, it felt like time was running out as the reluctant ghost faded.

The distance to Stephanie's door was under ten feet. Four good steps for a woman of Clara's height, but it took half of forever to tiptoe that distance when she had to stop and listen for the sound of feet on the stairs.

Heart racing, she nudged open the door and silently thanked Constance for running a well-oiled—literally— home.

Stephanie came awake with a start when Clara shook her shoulder.

"Shh. Don't make a sound. There's someone in the house and I need you to hide while I deal with him."

"Who?"

"I don't know," Clara practically dragged the younger woman out of bed and bundled her into a closet larger than her bedroom over Balms and Bygones. "Find a place to hide and stay there no matter what you hear, okay? I can handle this."

The first sound of stealthy footsteps sent Clara back into the bedroom Gathering herself for whatever was to come, she waited and listened for the sliding sound as the doorknob began to turn.

What would she do to keep Stephanie safe? How much magic could she use without running afoul of the harm-none rule? If there were lines to be drawn and then crossed, Clara would have to make those decisions on the fly. Most importantly, she trusted Roma to get to Mag and Mag to get help—of the human variety—here before she reached any point from which she could not return.

To that end, she drew from the pool of Balefire that was her family's birthright, and sent a flickering tongue of it into the doorknob.

A muffled exclamation followed the knob returning to its original position and Clara grinned. Round one to me, she thought. Let's see what's next on the roster. She could feel him there, on the other side of the door, and wished she had a hint of Roma's ability. How fun it would be to thrust her head through the door and say, "Boo!"

If she'd remembered to bring her charm bag, she would have been able to do more. It occurred to her then that she could have asked Roma to have Mag send the bag along. Clara could only call it to her if she knew its exact location, and Mag could have put it anywhere.

The doorknob rattled twice as if touched by a tentative finger to test for danger. She waited until it moved again, hit it with a level two blast, and listened for a reaction. Muffled cursing barely penetrated the thick door, but she'd bought herself a minute or two. Surely Roma would have rallied Mag by now.

In fact, Clara wondered why her sister hadn't shown up already. It wasn't like Mag to miss out on catching a bad guy, and she'd expected Roma to flit right back once the message was delivered.

Round three failed to deter the intruder, who must have wised up and wrapped something around his hand before turning the knob. It was too much to hope the hot knob would keep him stymied for long.

Running on pure instinct, Clara went with the first idea that came to mind, cast a glamour to turn dark hair to blond, and made a mad leap for the bed. She pulled up the covers just as the figure eased into the room.

Dark against dark, he kept to the shadows and approached the bed. When the hand reached past her to pick up a pillow, she still wasn't sure who stood over her with the intention to kill.

Roma materialized in Clara's living space with a popping sound. "Mag, you need to—" she trailed off when she got a good look around.

"Wanna drink?" Lounging on a reclining lawn chair in front of the Balefire, Mag waved a wine bottle in Roma's direction. Swirls of fringe marched up the arm of the free-love era suede jacket Clara would never let her wear in public. To complete the ensemble, she'd gone with a vintage tee that, on closer inspection, appeared to be autographed by half the performing lineup at Woodstock.

In the fireplace, the roaring Balefire spit sparks and cycled through a psychedelic series of colors. It was pretty, if mesmerizing, to watch. Sandalwood incense and sage leaves burned in several censors, smudging the air with smoke and scent.

"Cure what ails you," with an exaggerated head nod, Mag slurred the suggestion and tried to focus her eyes by opening them as wide as she could. When that didn't work, she squinted.

Dismayed, Roma said, "You're drunk."

"Lil bit." Mag agreed. "Don't tell Clara I found her stash."

To Mag's right, cuddled into a second lounge chair, an equally bleary-eyed Hagatha Crow cackled wildly and started repeating the word stash as if she'd never heard it before. The potent combination of faerie wine and powerful magic lowered the old witch's inhibitions—not that Hagatha's were all that strong to begin with. Sometime during the last half a century, she'd misplaced the bulk of her give-a-crap.

Based on her actions, she didn't seem to miss it, either.

"I need you to call the police and send them out to Huffington Manor. Can you do that?" Roma might as well have been talking to the lava lamp. "Mag, do you hear me? Clara's in trouble."

"Go 'way. Shoo."

Offended by the way Mag waved her off, Roma took matters into her own hands. "Whizzer! Come!" She called the ghost dog. "Where's the kitty? Go find Jinxie. That's a good boy."

Peeing on every surface wasn't the only reason Whizzer lived up to his name. Whiz certainly described the speed with which he made the rounds, and cornered Jinx in Clara's bedroom.

"Get off me you crazy dog," floated out of the room followed by the sound of two feet hitting the floor.

"Thank the stars." Roma said as he entered the room, "I need your help. Call the authorities and send them to Huffington Manor. Clara's in trouble. Hurry now—there's no time to waste."

"I'm sorry. I'm so sorry." The rough whisper fell over Clara while the pillow hovered over her face, but his was still in shadow. It could be John—she prayed to Hecate it wasn't. Would he really try to kill the woman he'd raised as his own? Clara's heart said no, but her heart had been wrong before.

The pillow began its descent, but Clara had wasted too many seconds trying to identify her assailant and he moved faster than she'd expected. He landed on her chest, knocked the wind out of her, and pushed the smothering cushion down hard.

Clara couldn't breathe, and the shock of it drove everything out of her head but the urge to try and buck him off.

Meanwhile, he continued to apologize and as her struggles decreased, his volume increased.

"I'm sorry." Either Clara was closer to death than she thought or she thought she heard the angels sing when she realized the man trying to kill her was not the man she wanted to date.

With the edge of oblivion rushing toward her, Clara reached for the easiest magic in her arsenal and clothed herself in Balefire. Mason Pangborn's proximity to her protected him from the flames, but he had no way of knowing that and leapt away screaming as if he really were on fire.

Clara rose like gravity was a mere inconvenience, turned a face flickering with both flame and fury on Mason, and ran through a list of possible spells to cast. Each one carrying a higher karmic debt than the last. But he'd killed and planned to kill again, and he deserved to pay.

As if fueled by her emotions, the Balefire raced over Clara's skin in a display that went from blue to blinding white.

"What are you—an angel or a demon?" Covering his eyes, Mason cowered at her feet. "Don't burn me. I didn't mean to kill him."

Later, Clara would admit to feeling let down that the mere sight of her had been enough to break Mason. Hexing him would have felt more satisfying. She let the Balefire die out with a puff.

"I have no idea what you're talking about. Sounds like you have a stain on your conscience and it's making you hallucinate. Who did you not mean to kill, Mason? Bradley Graham?"

"Yes, Yes. Brad. I never meant it to happen." He stared at her like he was trying to see under her skin to what might lie beneath.

"You meant to kill me, though." Stephanie stepped out of the closet and flicked on the lights. Caught in the act, Mason had two options and Clara almost hoped he'd choose the stupid one. If he tried to run, she could justify a hex after all. Something easy like a two-left feet curse. Just a temporary one to keep him from getting away.

Much to Clara's disappointment, he chose the anti-climactic option.

"How could you? After I treated you like family." Something caught Stephanie's eye, and she pulled the sleeve of her nightgown down over her hand for protection before reaching to pick up the item.

"And you intended to frame me with this." Careful to avoid leaving fingerprints, she turned her hand palm up to reveal a glass paperweight.

"What was the plan? Knock me out, plant the evidence, then stage a suicide? What could you possibly hope to gain?"

The sound of an approaching siren indicated Mag had come through on that front, at least.

"I only needed another month and everything would have been fine. I'd have put all the money back, and no one would have known a thing."

The whole sordid story came out in great detail, in part because Clara positioned herself over Chief Cobb's shoulder and every time Mason stalled or tried to backtrack, she let a little Balefire play over her hands or face, and he rushed to continue.

On the fateful day, Mason had received a phone call and agreed to an early morning meeting to discuss Brad's concerns. Thinking it had to do with Cheyenne's ridiculous plea for startup capital, Mason was blindsided when presented with proof he'd been embezzling funds.

"After the first bad investment, I thought I had a sure thing, but the second one went south on me, too. So I borrowed a little. Just enough to meet escrow on the house and office. I only needed one good payoff, and I'd be back in the black."

"Oh Mason, if you'd needed money, you could have asked. I'd have given you any amount. You didn't have to take everything." He had the grace to look ashamed when Stephanie's voice hitched.

It had been a short leap between borrowing enough to make a couple of payments, and using foundation money to try and reverse his losses.

"I thought I'd covered my tracks, but he had copies of the evidence and refused to see reason. He was going to go to Stephanie with proof, and I had to stop him. I wasn't in my right mind when it happened."

"What happened to Bradly Graham?" Cobb prodded.

"I don't think Stephanie needs to hear this. Come on, dear." Constance had come up with Cobb when he arrived, and she tried her best to drag Stephanie out of the room before Mason could tell his story.

"No, I need to know." Stephanie refused to budge, but gripped the housekeeper's hand tightly.

"We argued, and I agreed to come clean, then when he turned to leave, I picked up the paperweight from my desk and hit him on the head with it."

Through the rest of Mason's confession, Stephanie remained stoic. When he described the Port Harbor back alley where he dumped the body, and throwing Brad's wallet out the window when he found it in his car, she stared straight ahead.

But when Cobb slapped the cuffs on Mason, and prepared to lead him out, she rose from her seat, and walked deliberately over to him. Her eyes were burning holes of anger when she reared back and slapped him with all her might. Once, then twice while the police chief watched, but didn't interfere.

Huffingtons had always held sway in the town of Harmony, and from what Clara could tell, he thought Mason deserved it anyway.

Chapter Sixteen

"Please, stay one more night," Stephanie urged. Her eyes looked dark in a face paled by trauma, and Clara couldn't find a way to say no. Besides, there was Roma still hanging around in all her ghostly glory, and Mag nursing the world's worst magical hangover.

The pair of them had shown up about an hour after Cobb pulled out of the driveway with his prisoner. Mag looked like something scraped off the bottom of a shoe after a day at the carnival. She still had on the fringed jacket, and her hair stuck up on one side. But she was relatively sober, which was a miracle in and of itself.

Still, she was cranky and Clara thought going home sounded less fun by the minute.

"If you're certain we won't be a burden."

"Nonsense." Seeming eager to make amends for her earlier suspicions, Constance cast a worried eye over Stephanie. "You'll stay. I'll make a nice pot of soup."

Mag shot her sister a killing look, got back a smirk, and tried to make the best of the situation. "With dumplings?" If Constance made them, no doubt they'd be like succulent clouds of perfection.

"Of course." The deal was struck, and Mag couldn't complain when she slid a fork through the first dumpling and found it studded with fresh sage.

"Just like Granny used to make." With that high praise, Mag fed the yawning pit created by too much wine, not enough sleep, and the backlash from Hagatha's sober-up spell.

The evening slid by in a blur of conversation about anything other than the events of the previous night. Stephanie never mentioned Brad's name, but whenever she fell silent, her face slid into sorrowful lines and the others pulled her back into the mix.

By the time Constance took herself off to the kitchen to brew the evening tea, Stephanie's eyes were already drooping.

"I'm not sure I need it tonight." She held her protest until Constance was out of hearing. "It tastes like dirty dishrag. With hints of mint and licorice and not a granule of sugar allowed to soften the blow. But it helps me sleep."

For about an hour as it turned out. Just as Clara fell into a light doze, a series of shrieks lifted her off the bed and onto her feet, crouched and ready to do battle.

Having come through the adjoining bathroom, Mag popped through the door with pillow creases on her face, a wild look in her eyes, and a wand in her hand. Balefire sparks dribbled from the fingertips of her other hand.

"What's going on? Are you okay?"

"I'm fine." Storing away the image of her sister so she could poke fun at her later, Clara's feet hit the floor. "It's Stephanie."

Two long strides and Clara had just yanked open the door when the next scream came from the hallway and Stephanie stumbled toward her.

Tucked into Clara's bed, Stephanie brushed sweat-soaked hair back from her face and took a sip of cold water. "You don't understand, he's calling me. Every night. I thought it would stop once I knew what happened. Got closure. But it's the same. He sounds so scared and lost and alone. My heart is breaking and all I want to do is go to him."

Mag and Clara exchanged a worried look.

"He wouldn't want you to—" Trying to frame the sentence thoughtfully, Clara got her point across without saying anything else.

"Oh, I didn't mean it like that. It's just that it feels so real, like he's still here and I just can't find him."

"He might be." Roma's voice coming from right behind her ear made Mag jump and then scowl because she hated even the mere suggestion that she might be scared of anything.

As Roma passed by, Stephanie pulled the blanket more closely around her shoulders and shivered in the sudden chill.

"What do you mean?" Directing the question toward Roma, Mag forgot for a minute that Stephanie couldn't see or hear the ghost in the room.

"It's like he's not dead," Stephanie said.

"I don't think he's dead," Roma agreed.

Another look passed between the Balefire sisters before Mag nodded for Roma to follow her and left the room.

"You think I'm crazy, don't you? It's just like last time only it's not the same. Don't you see?"

Gently, Clara settled on the bed, picked up Stephanie's cold hand to chafe some warmth into it. "Tell me."

The floodgates opened and Stephanie described again for Clara the dreams she'd had after her parent's accident. "I dreaded going to sleep because I knew the dreams would come."

The poor thing must be terrified. "How did you get them to stop?"

"It's hard to remember, but I think I grew out of it after a year or so. It was during the summer, right before my fifteenth birthday. Uncle John thought a change of scenery might help, so he rented a cabin in Colorado. It was just the three of us. No doctors, no therapy. Just the peace and quiet of the lake and frogs singing us to sleep each night."

Her busy fingers picked the blanket then smoothed it back into place while Stephanie kept her gaze lowered. "It's the same now. I dread going to sleep, but these don't feel like nightmares. I can't really explain how, but it's different. Like another level. Real but not real—and I know that doesn't make any sense."

But it did make at least a little sense to Clara. If these dreams bordered on the prescient or prophetic, based on her limited experience, they'd come with plenty of psychic and emotional baggage. Divination was Mag's strong suit.

Speaking of Mag, she stepped back inside and motioned for Clara to join her by the door, where she hurried through an explanation of Roma's theory.

"She wants to talk to Stephanie herself," Mag said, "but hasn't been able to make contact without help."

Clara pulled a deep breath in through her nose and blew it out through her mouth. "If she's wrong, we're going to get that girl's hopes up for nothing. Are you sure you want to do this?"

Mag tilted her head to look past Clara to where the younger women huddled in the bed. "Roma's still hanging around. Doesn't that count for anything?"

"It does. Of course, it does."

"Okay, I've got ascension stone and plenty of selenite in my pack. Combined with a smudge of bay leaf, we should be able to give them a chance to communicate."

"You explain what's happening, I'll go down to the kitchen and find the bay." With that, Clara tagged out and let Mag handle Stephanie on her own.

Or not entirely on her own. Hovering nearby, Roma chattered. "Tell her I believe her. And that it's all going to be okay. She's sad. Give her a hug."

Until Mag snapped.

"Shut up. Just shut up."

Stephanie jumped at the sharp tone. "Was I talking? I'm sorry, I didn't realize."

Sucking in a breath through her nose and letting it out on a sigh, Mag would have waited for Clara to return if it weren't the coward's way out because what she was about to do had the potential to be either amazing or amazingly cruel.

"I'm sorry," she said. "I wasn't yelling at you. I was yelling at Roma. She's here and she has a crazy idea that she wants to talk to you about and we'd rather let her tell you in her own words." She outlined what it would take to make that happen, and finished going over it the third time just as Clara returned with a jar of bay leaves and a brass pot.

"Constance will kill us for this, but it's the only way." While Mag powered up the crystals and laid them out in a circle, Clara fed Balefire into the leaves until they started to smolder. When the cloud of smoke was dense enough, she set the pot beneath Roma's hovering feet in the center of the makeshift summoning ring.

As the old medium's features appeared in the smoke, Stephanie gasped and breathed her name.

"Can you hear me?" Roma asked.

"Yes, I can."

"These dreams you've been having—I don't think they're nightmares at all. I think Brad is caught between the physical world and the spiritual plane, and he's trying to make contact.'

Having stepped back to let Roma take the stage, Clara whispered to Mag, "I'm a witch with a willing suspension of disbelief and that sounds like hokum to me. What does that even mean? Caught between the worlds? Sounds like she thinks he's still alive."

"Shh. I think she's on to something."

Clara worried they were giving Stephanie false hope and at the end of the day, she'd be in worse shape than before. The only reason she didn't step in and put a stop to it was the simple fact that Roma had not gone, so something still remained of her unfinished business.

"What should I do?" Stephanie asked.

Roiling smoke hid Roma's features, but not her shrug. "Why, that's simple. Go back to sleep and see what he wants."

What little color that had come back to Stephanie's face drained away, but she closed her eyes and when she opened them again, they were filled with determination. "If it will help Brad, I'll do it. But you should know that I feel like I might never sleep again. My heart is pounding and my nerves are vibrating like the strings on my piano. Sleep is the last thing on my mind."

If they were going to go through with this, then Clara would pitch in and do her part. "Where does Constance keep her special tea? I'll go brew you a cup. While I'm gone, Mag can take you through a relaxing guided meditation."

Pointing out what she thought was the obvious solution, Mag said, "Or we could just cast a sleep spell over her."

"Might interfere with the psychic connection. We're better off to duplicate what she's been doing. Tea and natural sleep." At least she could protect Stephanie to that degree, Clara thought. If anything happened, the last thing the young woman needed was to be stuck in a spell-induced coma. "Help her relax and don't use any magic."

"She keeps it in a blue tin with roses on the lid, in the cabinet near the coffee pot."

Just before she sailed out the door, Clara spun to catch Mag in the act of making a face at her retreating back. "I saw that. Grow up, Maggie, before your face freezes like that."

The tomfoolery made Stephanie grin and the grin released some of the tension across her shoulders.

Still battling misgivings, Clara went downstairs and put the water on to heat while she searched for the tea. The box, a pretty thing that would have looked good on one of Mag's shelves in the store, was right where Stephanie said it would be. Popping the lid, Clara sniffed at the loose-leaf blend.

Mint, but not just peppermint. There were notes of spearmint and wintergreen as well.

A touch of anise for that licorice note Stephanie had mentioned. But the final two ingredients were the money shot. Melatonin and valerian root. A combination that, for someone with even a low-level psychic gift, could trigger some interesting side effects. Bad dreams or night terrors topped the list, with the possibility of hallucinations coming not too far behind.

Giving this tea to Stephanie would, at best, increase her psychic connection to Brad if he was trying to make contact, and at worst, send her on a wild goose chase through the land of wishful thinking. Neither scenario set well with Clara's conscience. Harm none applied to magic, but there was a line here that Clara had to decide if she could cross.

Still, she spooned the leaves into the tea ball and dropped it into the pot to steep. If Roma was right, Stephanie would want to help Brad, and even if nothing came of it but a sense of closure, Clara couldn't see the harm in letting her drink one more cup. One.

To ensure no more nightmares would rise from this particular brew, she crafted a little spell, fed Balefire into the tin until it glowed with blue light and chanted:

With good intent I make this charm

What is stored here do no harm

Satisfied, Clara put away the charmed tea tin and decided never to tell Stephanie what she'd learned. If the information ever got back to Constance, she would be heartbroken to learn she'd done more harm than good with her remedy.

After tonight, that danger would be gone. Clara carried the tea upstairs.

Chapter Seventeen

"This is crazy. Completely crazy," Stephanie repeated as she drank the tea Clara brewed.

"As crazy as you thinking you might have killed your fiancé?" Roma countered. "As crazy as talking to a ghost and inviting two witches to spend the night at your house? It might be time to reconsider your stance on the word. Your mother came to see me regularly because she believed. I think she would have raised you to be a believer too, if she'd had the chance. If I'm right, you have the gift, and it's what's been allowing you to connect with Brad."

"And if you're wrong?" Stephanie asked, swallowing hard.

Roma smiled. "I'm rarely wrong, dear. And if I happen to be this time, I think Mag and Clara will be here to help you through what comes next. What do you say we find out?"

Stephanie considered what Roma had said and nodded her assent, once again proving the strength of her constitution. Roma beamed, pride swelling in her bosom. "That's that, then."

Clara took a seat by the head of the bed, and spoke to Stephanie in soothing tones. "Relax, and find a comfortable position. Focus on your breathing. Count to four on the inhale, hold it for seven counts, and exhale for eight. The 4-7-8 method will slow your heart rate and allow you to fall into a deep sleep. Inhale, hold, exhale."

It took all of four minutes for Stephanie to doze off, leaving the others nothing to do but wait for a sign. When her eyes began to flicker beneath their lids, they knew she'd begun to dream.

On the other side of the veil, Stephanie discovered that accepting her dreams as reality helped clear the cobwebs. She let go of the doubts, the idea that she was insane, and embraced the fact that she might have actual powers of some sort. If it would help her figure out what had happened to her love, she'd have gladly believed she possessed the ability to sprout eyes in the back of her head.

Slowly, the world around her became more solid, grounded in reality as belief bolstered form.

"Brad!" she called out as she walked through a dream version of her backyard garden, bathed in color and light. Up ahead, she saw a figure standing next to the gypsy wagon her father had commissioned at her mother's request, and quickened her pace to catch up. This time, she wouldn't let him wander away. This time, she was in control.

"Stephanie!" Brad called back, splitting the distance between them in three quick strides. He pulled her against his chest and held her for a moment before looking into her eyes, "Is this real? What's happening? Am I dead?"

"I thought you were," Stephanie breathed through the tears that wet her face, "But now, I'm not sure. Tell me what you remember."

Brad was quiet for a minute, his eyes searching for something, "I remember finding something weird in the finances. And then talking to Mason, then pain, and then nothing. Until, well, this." He waved a hand to indicate the garden. "I've been waiting for you, but every time I catch a glimpse of you, you disappear. I thought it was a dream, but I can't seem to wake up, even though the voices keep telling me to."

"What voices?"

"I don't know," Brad said, shaking his head, "but none of them was you, and I was afraid."

"Of what?"

"I don't know," he repeated, "there was a light, and I could feel it there, waiting to be followed, but I was afraid if I left, you'd never find me. It doesn't make sense, I know."

"None of this makes sense," Stephanie replied, "but I think you have to follow the voices, wherever they lead. You're not dead—I'm more sure now than ever, or I wouldn't be able to talk to you. It's why Roma couldn't find you."

"Who's Roma?" Brad asked, confused again.

Stephanie grinned, "I'll explain everything, I promise. It's time for you to go and find the voices, I think." As soon as she said it, she realized it was true. The air around them had changed, the wind picking up and whipping her hair around her face and forcing her eyes closed.

When she opened them again, Brad was being pulled away from her, and the harder she tried to hold on the more difficult it became.

"I love you, Stephanie. For always." His voice died as he floated into the ether and disappeared. Stephanie felt as though her heart was breaking, and also healing at the same time, over and over again with each beat, and that was the last thought she had before diving back into the darkness.

Stephanie awoke to the sound of the phone ringing, her face still wet with tears. She didn't understand the look of bewilderment Mag and Clara exchanged until she realized it was the middle of the night and not a normal time for anyone to be calling.

Roma's transparent face lit up in a ghostly smile, and Stephanie jumped out of the bed and sprinted across the room at lightning speed.

"Hello?" She said into the receiver, listening for what felt like an hour to Mag and Clara, but was really only about ninety seconds.

"Oh my goodness. I'll be right there. Thank you!"

She turned around, beaming, and shouted, "He's alive! He's in the ICU at Port Harbor General. He's been in a coma all this time, and they thought he was someone else. There were two men found without identification at around the same time. Similar build, similar coloring."

Sometimes luck favored the criminal, and that had been the case with Mason.

"The nurse was very apologetic that they didn't try harder to identify Brad. The other man didn't make it. But he's alive. Roma—" Stephanie looked around the room, but the only people left in it were Mag and Clara.

"I'm sorry, honey. She's gone."

All the lights were on inside Huffington Manor when Mag and Clara pulled up in the long black limousine Stephanie had sent to retrieve them from Balms and Bygones. The sounds of music wafted into the driveway along with happy voices and laughter. In short, the place felt more alive than the Balefires had ever seen it.

But that was nothing compared to the difference they saw in Stephanie's demeanor when they entered through the front door and spotted her hanging on the arm of a handsome man who couldn't take his eyes off her.

"Mag! Clara! You're finally here!" She rushed over to greet the pair, the smile on her face enough to bring happy tears to Clara's eyes. Stephanie enveloped them in a Chanel-scented hug, towing Brad along behind her.

"These are the women who saved your life. And mine." Stephanie added for good measure, beaming as she made introductions.

"I can't thank you enough for everything you've done. You gave me my life back, Brad said."

Brad ignored the hand Clara held out and instead wrapped his arms around first her and then Mag, eliciting a giggle from the former and a tiny smile from the latter. It was more than Mag usually allowed, and whether she wanted to admit it or not, she found the young man rather charming.

"Maybe you could convince Constance we don't have designs on her tea service," she said once he'd released her.

His voice thick with emotion, Brad laughed, and thanked the two women again while they insisted they'd only done what any decent human being would do. "You're part of the family now, as far as we're concerned. Consider yourselves welcome anytime."

"More than welcome, actually. I expect to see the both of you here on a regular basis." Stephanie interjected. "Though, you'll only be visiting Constance and Cheyenne for the next month, because we've decided to bunk tradition and do this thing in reverse. We're leaving for an extended honeymoon next week. Brad set it up before everything happened." She lowered her voice and added, "That woman Cheyenne was so worried about—she's the travel agent Brad hired."

Mag nodded, genuinely glad to hear it, and even more happy that the last piece of the puzzle had finally slipped into place.

"Oh," Stephanie said in a low voice, "and tell that lady from your Moonstone Circle I'm happy to contribute some charitable funds to the organization, as long as she stops leaving messages on my voicemail. Quite persistent, that one."

Mag and Clara exchanged a bemused look. "Penelope," they said, rolling their eyes in unison.

"Yes, that's her. Tell me, is she a witch, too? I get the feeling there's more going on with those Moonstones than you'd like anyone to think." Stephanie winked conspiratorially and turned her attention back to her fiancé, pulled his head down, and rested her cheek prettily against his.

Clara's eyes were focused on watching the festivities happening around her when a feeling of compulsion overcame her. She turned around, searching the crowd until her gaze lit on John, who was watching her from across the room. Their eyes locked, and she made her way toward him with her heart in her throat.

"Hi." Clara said shyly, accepting the hug he offered while the pterodactyls in her belly whipped themselves into a frenzy.

"Hi, Clara," he replied. "You never called and I thought you might need some time. Things have been quite hectic around here the past few days. It's a relief to know Brad isn't who I thought he was. I'd been feeling so guilty," he blurted, then looked embarrassed at the admission.

"Guilty about what?" Clara asked, not sure she wanted to hear the answer.

"I lied. I did see Brad that morning, and I threatened him. Not with physical harm," John quickly qualified when he noticed the shocked expression on Clara's face. "I just said that if he was anything like his father, he needed to leave my niece alone or face the consequences. When he disappeared, I figured I'd been right and he'd taken the hint. I just didn't have the heart to tell Stephanie. It felt like adding insult to serious injury. I should have known it was the wrong line to take, but then things got out of hand and I was afraid she'd hate me for it."

That explained a lot.

It also went some way toward banishing the wall of reserve her intuition had built against him.

Returning warmth and the contrite expression on his face combined with the fact that she knew his intentions came from an honorable place absolved him in her mind. After all, who was she to judge? She had her own regrets, and they were far bigger than an unfounded accusation and a hollow threat.

"It's all come out in the wash." Clara said with an understanding smile." The best thing to do with guilt is turn it into a lesson learned. I'm just glad it's all worked out."

"So am I. I'm still not certain I fully understand what happened, but Stephanie insists you were responsible for finding Brad. We're all very grateful. I've never seen her so happy."

Clara smiled, watching the young couple interact. "It was my pleasure. What did she tell you, exactly?"

"Some ludicrous-sounding story about connecting with Brad through her dreams. I don't know if that's even possible, but she believes it, so who am I to judge?"

Clara's pulse sped up. Was it possible John might not be as closed off to the idea of magic as she thought he'd be?

"Is it really so crazy?" she hedged. "People have believed in the supernatural for as long as there have been people around to believe in anything."

John raised an eyebrow, "I suppose that's true. But the more things are explained by science, the less room there is for the supernatural. Just because we don't understand something, doesn't mean it's magic."

"Or, perhaps, science and magic are one and the same. There's magic all around us, every day."

"Well, I certainly feel something magical happening right now," he replied, pulling Clara to him and planting a sizzling kiss on her lips.

Oh, no, Clara thought to herself as she sank into him. *I'm in so much trouble.*

The End